WILD
THING
An Eddie Dancer Mystery

Mike Harrison

ECW Press

Published by ECW PRESS
2120 Queen Street East, Suite 200, Toronto, Ontario, Canada M4E 1E2

LIBRARY AND ARCHIVES CANADA CATALOGUING IN PUBLICATION

Harrison, Mike (Mike S.), 1945-
Wild thing / Mike Harrison.

(An Eddie Dancer mystery)
ISBN 1-55022-719-X

I. Title. II. Series.

PS8615.A749W54 2006 C813'.6 C2006-900296-7

Editor for the Press: Michael Holmes
Cover and Text Design: Tania Craan
Cover Image: Todd Gipstein/National Geographic Image Collection/
Getty Images
Typesetting: Mary Bowness
Printing: Friesens

This book is set in Sabon and Bubba Love

The publication of *Wild Thing* has been generously supported by the Canada Council, the Ontario Arts Council, and the Government of Canada through the Book Publishing Industry Development Program.

DISTRIBUTION
CANADA: Jaguar Book Group, 100 Armstrong Ave.,
Georgetown, ON L7G 5S4
UNITED STATES: Independent Publishers Group,
814 North Franklin St., Chicago, IL 60610

PRINTED AND BOUND IN CANADA

To Jan, Alec, and Annalisa, Gavin and Sarin

~

*With special thanks to Margaret Fergusson,
Andrew Fulcher, Kelly McLachlan, Trisha Coles,
Chris Podeski, and Janet Klippenstein*

Chapter One

WHEN THE PHONE ON my night table rang at 3:44 on Wednesday morning, I assumed that somebody had died. It wasn't an unnatural assumption, given my line of work.

"Hello?" I tried to sound respectful of the newly bereaved.

A man's voice came from a long way off.

"Edward?"

Nobody called me Edward. Except my parents, but they have been dead for ten years.

"Who's this?"

"It's Dr. Peter Maurice."

I searched my memory but didn't need to go back very far. Dr. Maurice headed up a team of specialists brought in to help me after a violent episode last summer. He was a psychologist of some renown, flown in from Vancouver to make sure my brain recovered the way brains should when they've been shaken, not stirred.

"How are you, Doctor?" It gave me a thrill to ask psychologists how they were. They never gave you a straight answer though.

"Fine," he lied. "Just fine."

"I'm glad to hear it."

It was now 3:46 in the morning. I remembered he was a long-winded old soul.

"So, are you fit and well and back on the job, Edward?"

"Hundred percent," I lied. "No longer a defective detective."

"That's very good to know." He paused. "Maybe I could use your services."

"My pleasure," I assured him. "Where are you?"

"In England," he said. "I'm under house arrest."

I let that sink in for a moment.

"Why?"

"Why am I in England, or why am I under house arrest?"

"Why are you under house arrest in England?" I played him at his own game.

"I'm here on a book tour," he said. "Promoting *Eye Too Eye* in the United Kingdom."

I had an autographed copy of *Eye Too Eye* in my bookcase downstairs. It was his take on what was wrong with the world. Chapter One said our problems all began with *too*. We either had *too much* of something, such as stress or work or time on our hands, or *too little* of something else, such as money or time or life skills. The secret, according to Chapter Two, was to achieve total congruency between the conscious and subconscious minds.

His words, not mine.

Chapter Three began to use words such as *sub-modalities, neurolinguistics* and *re-entrainment*.

I never reached Chapter Four. But as bad as it was, I didn't think it was grounds for house arrest.

"Are book tours illegal over there, then?" I asked.

"Well, no," he answered, seriously. "But apparently, the British police believe I'm a mass murderer. Their number one serial killer, in fact."

"Well, it's nice to be number one at something," I said. "And that would explain the house arrest," I added, relieved that it wasn't the quality of his book after all.

"Yes, indeed."

He could be quite droll.

"How can I help?"

"Can you come over? We really do need your help."

"Who's we?"

"My wife is with me."

"Coming over won't be a problem," I said, since I was, as we say in the profession, between jobs, "but how much help can I be, Peter? I don't know the country. I don't know their laws."

"I'll take that chance," he said. "My wife can organize your flight, book you a hotel. How soon can you leave?"

"How long do you need me for?"

"I don't know. Let me give you my phone number."

I scrambled out of bed. What sort of defective private detective was I not to keep a pen and paper on the bedside table in case a notorious serial killer called in the middle of the night? I hurried downstairs to the kitchen. The hardwood floor was cold on my bare feet. I grabbed a pen and paper from the drawer.

"Okay."

It was a long number that included the country code. I counted fifteen digits when I read them back to him.

"Can you let me know soon?" he asked.

"Why do they have you under house arrest? How come you're not in jail?"

"It's a temporary measure. They'll transfer me to jail later this week."

"Why do they think it's you?"

"Circumstantial evidence," he said. "But it's very persuasive. On the face of it, Edward, even I believe I'm guilty."

"But you're not?"

I had to ask.

He paused a short moment. It was a classy pause, born of neither guilt nor suspicion.

"No," he said, finally. "I'm most assuredly not."

Which was good enough for me.

"When's the next available flight?" I asked him.

"I'll let you talk to Sylvia."

The phone went dead for few long seconds and I listened to the sound of November snow melting from my roof and running through the eavestroughs. A chinook wind was blowing outside. I could hear it gusting hard against my little two-storey in Marda Loop, one of Calgary's more trendy areas. Chinooks are warm, moist Pacific winds that blow in hard over the Rocky Mountains. A dense blanket of low grey cloud obscures the sky and forms an impressive sky-blue chinook arch directly above the mountains. The warm air becomes trapped beneath this blanket of cloud and can raise the ground temperature by as much as twenty to thirty degrees in a matter of hours.

Chinooks play havoc with the barometric pressure, bestowing upon Calgary the dubious title of Migraine Capital of the World.

A woman's voice interrupted my thoughts of warm winds and migraine headaches.

"Hello, Edward?" She sounded strained.

"Hello, Sylvia."

"Peter is in trouble," she said. "He really needs your help."

"I'll do whatever I can," I promised. "Have you had time to check on any flights?"

"Yes. That's why we called you so early. There is a flight out of Calgary at 7:45 a.m. Your time. Can you be on it?"

Four hours. I did a fast mental locate of my belongings. Passport. Underwear. Toothbrush.

"Sure."

"Oh, thank you," she said, her relief evident. "I have reserved a seat in your name. With Peter's credit card. You'll need to take a cab from the airport when you get here."

"I land at Heathrow?"

"Yes."

"And where are you?"

"In a place called Saint Albans."

"What's your address?"

She gave me the address and said she had booked me in at the Queens Hotel. I wrote it all down. The flight was due at Heathrow around midnight their time.

"Can you get me a late check-in at the Queens?"

"Yes, of course."

"I'm on the way, then."

"Just a minute. Here's Peter."

She handed the phone to her husband.

"Edward?"

"Yes, Peter?"

"I want you to know I really appreciate your help," he said.

"You're very welcome," I told him. "Now get off the phone. I have underwear to pack."

After we hung up, I made a pot of strong coffee. I thought about England. It had been more than ten years since I was last there. Maybe this time I'd get to try some of their famous figgy pudding.

I began packing for a cold British winter.

One without the benefit of warm chinooks.

Chapter Two

MY HAIR WAS STILL WET from the shower but I was packed and ready to leave by 4:37 a.m.

After I set the house alarm, turned down the thermostat ten degrees and phoned my answering service to let them know I'd be abroad until further notice, there was nothing left to do. I had no cats to cuddle, dogs to romp, fish to feed, birds to cage, nor elderly relatives over which to dote.

I live a singular and frugal existence.

I took a yellow cab to the airport and we used forty gallons of wiper fluid to keep the windshield clear.

The other downside of chinooks.

The international terminal was full of sleepy-looking travellers in need of a hearty breakfast. The ticket the Maurices bought me was first-class, so I avoided the crowds and was ushered aboard like Canadian royalty.

King Eddie.

They gave me a window seat, which was nice, but sat me next to an anti-social lady from the thirteenth century, laden with sufficient jewellery to seriously compromise our takeoff speed. She wore dozens of metal bracelets on both arms and it sounded like a serious engine malfunction every time she scratched.

Once we were in the air, I asked to borrow a map of Great Britain. The flight attendant lent me a hefty, battered old atlas. I hoped it wasn't the pilot's. Saint Albans was spelled St. Albans and was in the county of Hertfordshire, north of London. I measured the distance from the airport. Heathrow was west of London. It didn't look too far but I knew the traffic would be heavy and forty-odd miles could easily take several hours.

Before boarding, I'd phoned the lovely Cindy Palmer at home. I used one of the airport's pay phones. I had called her before I left Canada because I knew my cell phone wouldn't work in the United Kingdom.

Her answering machine kicked in right away, so I knew she was asleep. She's an E.R. nurse and works funny hours. Not as funny as mine, of course. I left her a cryptic message about Queen and country and told her machine I'd call it back tomorrow.

Then I covered the mouthpiece and whispered something sweet and syrupy and unambiguously sexual.

Which is what you do when the love-bug bites.

I left a more mundane message on Danny Many-Guns' answering machine. Danny's my sometime partner, my pick-up guy, my backup singer when things get a little too hot. One never knows where Danny might be, but I left him a message anyway.

"I'm on my way to Merrie England," I said. "Peter

Maurice needs some help. Dr. Peter Maurice," I added, in case he'd forgotten who Peter Maurice was, which was superfluous since Danny never forgets anything.

Somewhere over the Arctic, I tried to sleep, my head cradled in a pillow wedged against the window. But the best I could manage was a series of catnaps, interrupted by the Queen of Bling who'd developed a rash loud enough to wake the dead.

I thought about what Dr. Maurice had told me. Or hadn't told me. I wondered how something as civilized as a book tour could turn into a serial killer slugfest. Then I fretted about not being able to bring my gun with me. But a 9mm SIG Sauer isn't the kind of walk-on luggage Air Canada encourages. Besides, the Brits are funny about people walking around their island with a gun strapped to their thigh. I keep my gun padlocked inside a steel cabinet, behind a locked door in my basement, three locks between it and the outside world, as required by law, for I am nothing if not a law-abiding private detective.

Yeah, right.

I keep it in my night table where it will come in very handy should I need to shoot somebody in the head if they break into my house.

When I left Calgary, the temperature was hovering around plus six. Balmy by Calgary standards. When I arrived at Heathrow, the temperature, after a hasty conversion, was about minus two.

But it seemed like minus forty-two.

How the hell do these people survive? The air was damp and extremely chilly. Unless the cabbies kept their engines running, their windshields, pardon me, their windscreens, would ice up in minutes.

Clearing customs was the usual joy. Three customs agents, whose job was to slow the line flow, gave me the third degree.

I decided to lie when they asked about the purpose of my visit.

"Vacation," I told them, since, "I'm gonna spring a mass murderer from de clink," might have slowed the line down considerably more.

"You have no return ticket," they said, accusatorily.

"No, I don't," I agreed with them. "Why is that a problem?"

They huddled for a discussion, but when I pointed out the longer I stayed, the more money I'd spend, they grudgingly allowed me to set foot on their tiny, rain-drenched island.

Actually, Britain only pretends to be tiny.

But there's no pretense about it being rain-drenched.

I had a debate with a cabbie about how much he was going to charge to drive me to St. Albans. It was strange hearing a Cockney accent from a man in a turban. I have Cockney friends back in Calgary, so I was familiar with the dialect. I haggled the price from outrageous down to merely reprehensible and stowed my bags in the trunk.

Pardon me.

The boot.

Like I said, this wasn't my first visit to England. I'd spent time touring the U.K. more than a decade ago, the year before my parents died.

And the Brits still drove on the wrong side of the road.

My cabbie's name was Cecil and he was sulking because I told him I would shoot him if he lit the cigarette he'd just put in his mouth.

He didn't know my gun was in my bedside table.

The drive to St. Albans took just over two hours, most of it in moody but smoke-free silence. Cecil dropped me off outside the Queens Hotel just off St. Peter's Street, the main drag, and grumbled when I offered my Visa card. I hadn't had time to change dollars to Euros. He popped the boot lid from inside the cab and lit up, leaving me to wrestle my suitcase alone in the rain.

After I'd tipped him, of course.

The fifteen-second slog to the hotel's front entrance felt like a trip across the Arctic Circle. The hotel lobby was small but warm and comfortable, with matching flowery chesterfields and a coffee table stacked with magazines about horses. The reception desk was an ancient slab of polished mahogany reflecting a noisy ceiling fan that turned in cranky circles high above my head. Across from reception, a small fire spluttered in a large grate.

I pinged the brass bell on the desk, and a rosy-cheeked girl in her late teens appeared moments later.

"'Ello," she said brightly. "You must be Mr. Dancer."

"And you must be the Queen," I replied, though I didn't quite curtsy.

"No, silly," she said as if it were a common mistake, "she's up at Buckingham Palace. Now, if you could just fill in the 'otel registration." She produced a beige card. "No need to fill in the credit information. The room's already paid for." She turned away to get my key. "And there's a message for you, " she said and slid a small, white envelope across the countertop.

I pocketed the envelope, filled in the registration card and handed it back to her.

She read it.

"Ooh. Canada. I've always wanted to go there."

"It's a lot warmer than St. Albans," I told her, but she looked like she didn't believe me. I think I now know why they have such rosy cheeks, though. It's all of that rubbing to keep them warm.

"Do you need a hand up with your luggage, sir?"

I looked at my one small suitcase.

"I think I might manage," I said.

"Oh, good," she said, "only 'Enry's having a kip out back and it's the dickens to wake him."

I know that's what she'd said but I had no idea what she meant. Since it didn't seem to require an answer, I picked up my suitcase and followed her outstretched finger to the stairs.

"No elevator?" I asked.

"No," she said. "Do you have lifts in Canada?"

Lifts?

"No, I don't believe we do," I said. "Not much call for them in the igloos."

I carried my luggage up four flights of stairs and found my room at the far end of the hall. They really liked flowery wallpaper at the Queens Hotel. Flowery carpets, too. My room resembled an overgrown greenhouse, the bedspread a riot of flowers. Or maybe they were English weeds.

I left my suitcase at the foot of the bed and used the bathroom, which felt cold and damp. I sure hoped I could wrap this thing up quickly.

The note inside the envelope, in big, scrawly handwriting, incongruous on pale pink notepaper, said, "Edward. Please call me no matter how late you arrive." Beneath that was the phone number Peter had given me when they called me in Calgary. It was signed, "Dr. Peter Maurice," so I wouldn't confuse him with that other British serial killer, Dr. Harold Shipman.

The room phone was one of those big, black monstrosities you see in old movies. I think we should bring them back. It's so satisfying to hang up on telephone canvassers. You can really slam that thing into the cradle. It took me a moment to remember how to use the dial but I managed.

"Hello?" A man's voice.

"I've arrived," I said.

"Thank God." It was Peter. "Things have taken a turn for the worse. I'm being taken into custody in a few hours."

"They give you notice?"

"They are nothing if not polite."

"Maybe I should come over right now." I hoped he would register my lack of enthusiasm. I needed bed rest.

And lots of it.

"That would be best," he said. "You have the address?"

"I do."

"There's a policeman guarding the front door. Tell him you are here under my jurisprudence."

"They really talk like that?"

"Yes," he said. "They really do."

I hung up and went to the lobby, rehearsing my lines.

"'Ello again." The rosy-cheeked receptionist smiled brightly. "Can't sleep?"

"'Fraid not," I said. "Can you call me a cab?"

"A cab?"

"A taxi?"

"Oh." She giggled. "A cab. That's *so* American." She stretched forward over the desk and peered through the main door. I tried not to be impressed by her British cleavage. "You're in luck," she said. "There's one right outside."

I thanked her and hurried into the cold and the rain to hail the cab.

I hoped the cabbie wasn't moody Cecil.

Chapter Three

IT WASN'T.

My new cabbie was a very large white guy with really bad body odour. The good news was that the cab ride took just under a minute. I could have walked it faster. The cabbie made a big production of using my Visa, and when he drove away, I heard him complaining rather loudly, "Bloody Yanks."

As I crossed the street to Peter's rented house, I noticed a pair of dark figures huddled around a motorcycle near a street lamp. One of them twisted towards me and turned the darkness into daylight in the brilliance of a microsecond. I heard the whine of a camera motor and turned away from him. The next flashbulb lit up the back of my head.

Ah. The price of fame.

A tall wooden gate was set in a high brick wall that surrounded Peter's property. I unlatched the gate and stepped inside. The couple by the motorbike lost interest in me. I moved quickly up the narrow footpath to the front door.

A wet and sad-looking policeman was lurking in the shadows.

"Jurisprudence," I said as he stepped out of the undergrowth.

"Beg pardon, sir?" he enquired politely.

"Jurisprudence," I said, louder and more slowly, the way you do with foreigners, but he showed little sign of understanding. Maybe they pronounced it differently in England.

He leaned in towards me a little and cocked his head.

"What's that mean, then, sir?" he asked.

"Don't have a clue, actually." I shrugged.

"What do you want, then?"

"Dr. Maurice is expecting me."

"Well, why didn't you say that in the first place?"

He knocked on the door, and when Peter Maurice opened it, the policeman announced me.

"You have a visitor, Dr. Maurice."

"Edward." Peter looked relieved to see me.

I stepped inside and Peter closed the door behind me. We shook hands and then, being Canadian, I took off my shoes. I hung my coat on an impressive-looking hat stand and followed Peter into the kitchen in my stocking feet. A woman was standing with her back to me, looking out the window. A tall, slim woman standing very still.

"This is my wife, Sylvia," he said.

She turned to face me. She looked younger than she'd sounded on the phone. Much younger than Dr. Maurice. Very blonde, trim, well dressed in a beige skirt and matching blouse. She had a stylish, natural elegance and I had no doubt she'd been a model. Still could be. Great legs, high cheekbones and a slight overbite. Her skin was flawless, her eyes smoky grey in the kitchen light. Up close, I could see tiny worry lines radiating from the corners of those smoke-grey eyes. I shook her hand with both of mine and assured her that everything was going to work out fine.

We sat at the breakfast bar with a view over the back garden before Sylvia pulled the drapes closed.

"It's the police," she said. "They have men all around the house, looking in."

"Someone got a shot of me outside," I said.

"I'm sorry," she said, as though it was all her fault. "Are you hungry, Edward?"

"No, thank you."

"Coffee, then?"

"Coffee's fine," I told her.

While she poured the coffee, I studied Dr. Maurice. He looked good, considering. In his early fifties, a little more grey round the temples than I remembered, bushy eyebrows curling up towards his hairline, a salt and pepper beard trimmed to within a quarter inch. He looked to be in good shape, no extra fat, good eyesight since he didn't wear glasses. He wore dark slacks with a sharp crease and a white shirt under a tidy maroon V-neck sweater, even though it was well past three in the morning and he should have been in his jammies.

"Okay." I sipped my coffee. "So start from the beginning, Peter. I'll jump in if I have any questions."

He looked away, putting his thoughts in order.

"About three weeks ago," he began, "I received a letter from a young woman living here in England."

"Do you have it?"

"I have a copy, yes. The RCMP entered my home in Vancouver and faxed a copy to the British police a few days ago. I had them forward me a copy. My lawyer suggested I do that."

"Did you know this woman?"

"No. I'd never heard of her until the letter arrived. I was intrigued so I phoned her."

"In England?"

"Yes. I told her I was coming over on a book tour, which she knew about, of course, and we arranged to meet."

"Why 'of course'?"

"Because that was why she had written to me, specifically."

"What did the letter say?" I asked.

He turned to his wife. She had anticipated his request. She took a copy of the letter from a file folder sitting on the kitchen table and handed it to me.

"You should maybe read it first," she said and turned to Peter. "It will make more sense to him if he does." She turned to me. "We'll wait for you in the drawing room. It's more comfortable."

"Yes," Peter agreed. "Read the letter. We'll wait for you."

Sylvia picked up the slim file folder and tucked it beneath her arm. She led the way and Peter followed her out of the kitchen.

I hoped they'd come and get me when I was finished. I had no idea what a drawing room looked like. I sat at the breakfast bar and laid the letter on the countertop. Three unlined pages of neat handwriting, the lines all perfectly straight; a skill I had never mastered. The letter was addressed to Peter at his home in Vancouver. I took another sip of coffee and began reading.

Chapter Four

Dear Dr. Maurice,

My name is Maria Glossard and I live in Crawley, in the south of England. I am married and have a two-year-old baby boy we call Evan. My husband's name is Eric. Glossard is, of course, my married name. My maiden name was Tailor but I am directly related to the Mesmer family. I am, in fact, the great-granddaughter (several times over) of Dr. Franz-Anton Mesmer, the Austrian physician who, many believe, was the founding father of hypnosis. My mother died when I was very young. She and my father had already split up and I was raised by my grandmother in Meersburg, a small town in Germany. We lived in the very same (and very small!) house where Great-grandpa Mesmer had lived almost two hundred years ago. He came to Meersburg to retire, and died, as you know, a very poor man. The only thing he had left was his house. It has stayed in the family ever since. This past July, my grandmother died of emphysema. She was seventy-one when she passed away and I am her only living relative. In her will, she left me the house and all of its contents. My husband and I decided to take Evan with us for a holiday and we drove to Meersburg to look the place over. We stayed at the house to save on hotel bills. It was in worse shape than I remembered and we both felt that it would be best to sell it and use the money to help pay down our mortgage here in England. We sorted through the furniture and I salvaged a few pieces of sentimental value. The rest we gave to charity. The local real estate office appraised it (it was worth even less than we expected) and I agreed to list it for sale once all the paperwork had been completed. The lawyer over there informed us we would receive some money from the house but much of it would be eaten up in taxes.

The day we were leaving, Eric decided to check out the attic. It had rained heavily the night before and he wanted to make sure that the roof wasn't leaking. There was only the tiniest ceiling hatch in the upstairs bedroom ceiling but Eric is very slim and managed to wiggle his way through (tearing his trousers in the process!).

In the attic, beside the chimney in a dark corner, he found a small brown paper parcel, thick with dust. So thick, in fact, he almost didn't see it. He lowered it down to me and we brushed off the dust in the bathtub. The bundle was tied together with twine and there was a red wax seal over the knot. It looked like something had been pressed into the wax and when we cleaned it, we could clearly see the letter M. Eric said it was probably Mesmer's personal seal.

We were very curious to see what was inside so we cut the string rather than break the seal. Inside, we found a stack of handwritten brown parchment paper sheets. About thirty pages in all. But they were written in Italian. Old Italian. Although Grandpa was fluent in German, French and English, he much preferred Italian. Since I can only speak a little German, reading his manuscript was beyond me.

Clearly, though, these were the handwritten notes of my great-great-grandfather, Dr. Mesmer. I understood them to be his research notes, research notes that hadn't been seen in almost two hundred years.

Since we weren't going to be seeing much money from the house, and what little we would see would take quite a while to materialize, we decided to take the manuscript home with us in the hopes of selling it. We didn't think of it as actually smuggling but, better safe than sorry, we sewed it into the baby's mattress for safekeeping.

Before we left, we visited Mesmer's memorial at the local cemetery. It was designed by Professor Karl Christian Wolfart, Dr. Mesmer's closest friend, and it was very beautiful. I knew, then, that taking the papers was the right thing to do, as I'm sure my Great-grandpa would have wanted them to be published.

When we got back home, we tried to get the manuscript translated but people began asking too many questions and we decided to forget about it for a while. Evan became ill shortly after we got home and then, just last month, Eric broke his leg, so we had enough on our plate for the time being and put it on the back burner.

Then I saw a copy of your book, Eye Too Eye, *and just had to read it. I loved your tribute to my great-grandfather. It was very moving.*

And that is why I decided to write you this letter. Dr. Maurice, would you be interested in purchasing Dr. Mesmer's manuscript? I think his research notes could be of value and we are only looking for a modest sum, certainly less than the manuscript is probably worth. I read that you are coming to England soon as part of your book tour. Perhaps we could meet?

Yours very sincerely,
Maria Glossard

Chapter Five

PETER HAD INDEED DEDICATED his book to Dr. Franz-Anton Mesmer. He wrote about Mesmer's commitment to the healing life and the injustices he had suffered in the name of medicine. It was quite moving and it obviously had a profound effect on Maria Glossard.

I went in search of the drawing room and was disappointed to discover it looked just like a living room. A baby grand took up space near the window. The surrounding walls were hung with oil paintings of overly jolly-looking fat men with red jackets and rosy cheeks, sitting astride improbably large horses, chasing evil-looking foxes. This was clearly a reflection of the painter's bias, since foxes are really rather cute. The furniture was plump and comfy and Peter and Sylvia sat side by side on one of two chesterfields. They looked at me with an expectant air, as though I'd come to play them a piano recital.

"You read the letter?" Peter asked.

"Yes. I'm just not sure of the connection."

"Maria Glossard was murdered ten days ago, two days

after we arrived here. Her son, Evan, was also killed. It was the first in a series of terrible murders throughout southern England. In all, ten women have been killed. The police believe I did it."

"That's a murder a day," I said. "Do the police believe you killed them all?"

"Yes."

"How did they die?"

"Very badly." Sylvia spoke for the victims. "Their heads were crushed. The police think whoever did it carried some kind of apparatus around with him. Something powerful enough to inflict a lot of damage."

An apparatus.

To crush a woman's skull.

Some people have way too much time on their hands.

"And a lot of the women were also raped," Sylvia added.

"Why do they think it's you?" I asked Peter.

"Maria lived in a place called Crawley, a small town south of London, halfway to Brighton on the south coast. My book tour began in Brighton, so I was reasonably close. And I had planned to meet with Maria the following day."

"The day she was killed?" I asked.

"No. It was the day after. She was killed late the previous night."

"She talks about a husband," I said.

He shook his head.

"The police cleared him right from the start," Peter said. "He's a baker. He was working the night shift. Six witnesses. And he couldn't have done it because he has a broken leg. Someone has to pick him up and drive him home after his shift. It wasn't him."

"So you didn't see her?"

"No. We never met."

"What about the rest of the women?

"Here." He handed me a flyer from the folder they had taken from the kitchen. "This is my book tour itinerary. Dates, times and places. It's a copy of an advertisement my publisher placed in different newspapers and magazines."

I took the flyer. Peter's picture ran across the top, below that, his name and the title of the book and an invite to "meet the author." The bottom half comprised a list of maybe forty towns, many of which I'd never heard of before. I scanned them at random. Brighton. Crawley. Bognor Regis. Guilford. Sevenoaks. Slough. Watford. Barnet.

Some had been circled.

I counted the circles.

There were ten.

"So," I ventured, "the women who were killed all lived along the book tour route?"

"Most of them. Some worked in the same towns, others lived close by," he said, sadly.

"And they were murdered around the time you were passing through?"

"Exactly the time I was passing through."

"All of them?"

"Every one of them."

"So the cops put one and one together and came up with you."

"Yes." He looked uncomfortable.

"Did they know you had planned to meet Maria?"

"Eventually they did. You see, Maria cancelled the meeting. She phoned me at the bookstore down in Brighton the day before we were supposed to meet. Her son was really sick. She was actually in the emergency room at the local hospital when she called. So she mailed the manuscript to me. I told her to mail it care of the St. Albans post office and I'd pick it up there. The police found a receipt from the Crawley post office in her house. They traced it to me but didn't have an address, no way to contact me. Eventually, somebody made the connection between the dead women and the towns on my tour."

"Didn't you make the connection yourself?" I asked him.

"No." He shook his head. "I was on a pretty tight schedule most of the time. It was usually fairly late when I got back to the house. Once or twice, I actually stayed at a hotel but I preferred coming back here. Quite frankly, I wasn't watching television or reading the newspapers. World War Three could have broken out and I would have been oblivious."

I turned to Sylvia.

"Were you here too?"

"No. I only came over a few days ago. We were planning a vacation after the tour."

"Wasn't it a long drive back here every night, Peter?"

"It was, but I've been working on the sequel to the book and I found it easier to work in the same environment. I'm not much of a nomad, I'm afraid. My publisher rented this place for me."

"Do you have the manuscript? The one Maria sent?"

He shook his head. "No. The police have it. They claim it's an important piece of evidence."

I saw Sylvia turn and look at him but he refused to meet her eye.

"You have a lawyer here in England?"

"Yes. Geoffrey Lansdale. He has an office here in town. He's very . . . " he paused a moment ". . . thorough."

"Yet you're being arrested? Taken away and locked up?"

Sylvia coughed, maybe to cover a cry caught in her throat. Peter looked ashen. Well, he didn't hire me to hold his hand.

"I'm supposed to be touring the north of England starting tomorrow. We have another thirty-four cities on the tour."

"What's your publisher have to say about it?"

"Nigel? He thinks, and I quote, 'It's the best thing since sliced bread.' They are already into their third printing. Since my name was associated with the murders, sales of the book have really begun to climb."

"Who knows about the manuscript?" I asked.

"Well, the police do, of course," he said. "And Sylvia. You. And anyone whom Maria or her husband might have told. Though she did say they hadn't told anyone."

"You didn't tell your publisher?"

"No. I hadn't seen the material so I wasn't going to bring it up with them until I'd had time to study it. It might have been a hoax."

"It still might," I said.

"I don't think so. They weren't exactly asking a fortune and it has a ring of truth about it. Also, I talked with Maria on the phone and I believe I'm a good judge of character."

I could hardly deny that.

He'd hired me, after all.

"Could it be worth more than she was asking?"

He thought about that. Thought about it as a possible motive for murder.

"I don't know," he said. "Without seeing it, it's hard to judge. I just can't imagine what a two-hundred-year-old manuscript has to do with ten women being murdered."

"Maybe nothing at all," I said. "Maybe it has to do with your book."

"*Eye Too Eye?* I don't see how."

"Another writer? Jealous of your success?"

He smiled.

"Hardly," he said. "Until my name became linked with the murders, the book wasn't exactly setting any sales records, Edward. Besides, it's just not —" he searched for the right word "— plausible that it would be another writer. I think you're mixing nonfiction with the world of fiction."

"So what's your take on it, Peter? Who's setting you up?"

"If only I knew." He threw up his hands. "I've been over it a hundred times. I don't see any connection whatsoever. I think some psychopath has gotten ahold of my tour list and decided it would be fun to follow me around, murdering people."

"You don't think there's a connection between the manuscript and the murders?" I tried again.

"I don't know. The police certainly think so."

"When are they coming for you?"

He glanced at his watch. "My lawyer will be here by eight. We're expecting them by nine. They will be holding me at the St. Albans main police station for now."

I nodded. I sat still for a while, feeling jet-lagged and plain old bagged. I couldn't quite process everything he had told me.

"Don't suppose you have a photocopier here," I said. "I'd like to get a copy of the letter. And the tour list."

"There is a fax machine," Sylvia said. "I can make you a copy of both."

She took the originals with her, and Peter and I sat in silence until I thought of something else to say.

"You spoke with Maria just the one time?" I asked him.

"We spoke on the phone twice, actually. Once before I left Vancouver and again when she phoned the bookstore to cancel."

"How did she sound?"

"Fine. Upset, of course. She was disappointed because she was quite looking forward to meeting with me. Plus her son was really quite ill."

I found it odd that he put himself ahead of Maria's son in terms of her disappointment.

"How much did she want?" I asked.

"We had agreed on three thousand pounds. About six thousand dollars. Not an unreasonable amount. I mailed her a cheque for half that from Vancouver. I was planning to pay her the balance when I met with her. I still have the cheque for the other half."

"The first cheque was cashed?"

"I'm not sure."

Sylvia returned with my copies.

"Did the Glossards cash the first cheque?" he asked her.

"Yes. Three or four days before she was murdered."

"Cashed by Maria?" I said.

"I assume so," she said. "It was made out to them both." She paused. "Do you think the money had anything to do with it?"

"Who knows?" I shrugged.

"Someone would do that for fifteen hundred pounds?" she asked in disbelief.

"Some people would do that and worse for five," I said. "But it doesn't explain why the other nine women were murdered." I turned to Peter. "Have you spoken with her husband?" I asked.

"No. I wanted to but my lawyer advised against it."

We sat in silence for a while. Obviously, the first thing I needed to do was to meet with Maria's husband, Eric. Maybe he could shed some light on a few things.

"How did Maria's son die?"

Peter looked at the floor before answering. He didn't like discussing violence.

"He was suffocated," he said.

"But not sexually abused?" I asked because it might be important.

"I don't think so." He shook his head slowly. "I'm sure we would have heard if he had been. I think he was killed because he was there, with Maria, in the house. Wrong place, wrong time."

I sat there looking at them and wondered how they were holding up. The accusations alone were enough to shatter their lives.

"Peter." I leaned forward to get his attention. "Professionally, what makes someone do what this person has done? Could there be more than one of them?"

He closed his eyes a moment, digging into his vast knowledge of human behaviour.

"We all tend to do things to justify subconscious beliefs," he said. "Regardless of whether those beliefs are right or wrong, if we believe something, we will act accordingly. This man, and I say man because I really doubt there are two people, this man kills women because he believes they have wronged him in some monumental way and he's seeking revenge. Not each specific woman, because it's doubtful he would have known them personally. He goes after a specific type of woman, a type he identifies with the woman who wronged him. He prefers dark-haired women. Under forty. And fairly slim. Believe me, since the police came calling, I've read everything there is to read about the murders." I thought he was finished but he wasn't. "When he commits the murder, he takes his time. It is obviously important to him to prolong their pain for an extended period. It takes a lot to crush a person's skull. The pain is unbearable. That's his signature, not his modus operandi. You understand the difference?"

I did but I was always willing to learn more.

"Tell me," I said.

"His M.O. is his methodology. It's what he does and the order in which he does it. And it's how he gets away with it. It never really changes but it can evolve, he can refine his M.O. His signature, on the other hand, has nothing to do with the crime per se. His signature is what satisfies him in a deeply personal way. It's the satisfaction he receives from committing the act. Prolonging the victim's pain would seem to be his signature and it's driven by his psychological needs. Perhaps even by his fantasies. To put it crudely, his signature is what gets him off."

The room went quiet for a while.

"You say he's seeking revenge. Revenge for what?"

He shrugged. "A perceived injustice. It's retaliation for a pain he feels he has suffered. His justification in an unshakeable but irrational belief."

I waited to see if there was more, but he was spent.

I stood up slowly and stretched.

"I'm going to need a few hours' sleep," I said. "Then, I'm going to track down Eric Glossard. I want to talk with him, face to face. After that, I'll come back and find you."

"Would you give him this? It's the balance of what I owe them."

He handed me an envelope with a cheque inside.

"I don't think you're expected to pay the balance until you receive the manuscript," I said.

"Nonetheless."

He held the envelope out and I took it from him. Then he stood up and shook my hand.

"I have a great deal of faith in you, Edward. I saw how you recovered from that horrible ordeal back in the summer. You have great inner strength."

Sylvia was watching me.

"Thank you, Peter. I'll do my best."

"Peter?" Sylvia spoke softly.

He turned to his wife. She raised an eyebrow.

"Gosh, I almost forgot," he said. "Edward, there's no

point you staying at the hotel after tonight. This house has more than enough room for the three of us. If you're comfortable staying here, we'll arrange to have your things shipped over later today."

I looked at Sylvia. She was nodding. Perhaps she felt vulnerable on her own.

"That's fine," I said. "I'll be keeping very odd hours, though."

"We're used to that." Peter spoke as though he would be here, not languishing in a prison cell. "That's settled, then."

There was nothing left to do but say goodbye.

"I'll call you a taxi," Peter offered.

"I'll be in bed and asleep before it even gets here," I told him.

I took my coat from the hat stand and noticed a woollen ski mask, or balaclava, amid an array of mittens and scarves.

"Do you mind?" I asked him.

He shook his head, and I pulled the woollen mask over my head, adjusted the eyeholes and checked myself in the mirror.

I looked like a bank robber as I stepped outside.

The bored young copper was still lurking in the bushes, freezing his ass off.

Make that his arse.

"I'm off to a nice warm bed," I told him.

I have a real resentment towards authority figures. Maybe I should talk to Peter about it.

"Good for you, sir," the young officer said, sneering.

"And a nice hot cup of cocoa," I added, rubbing it in.

It was fun teasing the hired help.

"Very good, sir." He sounded resentful.

I think he resented the fashionable comfort of my ski mask. As I walked towards the gate, I heard him mutter quite clearly, "Bleedin' Canucks."

Outside, the dark shadows moved quickly. As I turned to walk up the hill towards the hotel, I heard the motorcycle engine fire up. The high beam swept the road ahead, and the bike drew level. The guy on the back turned sideways, pointed his camera at me and fired a barrage of shots, the strobe-like flash almost blinding me.

I looked at him and saw his disappointment. All he got was a pair of eyes. He tapped the rider on the shoulder and they turned away quickly.

Funny thing.

They didn't look like cops.

I rolled the balaclava up and wore it like a toque when I got to the hotel. The receptionist was still there and she smiled brightly and gave me a message as I crossed the lobby.

"You're to phone Mrs. Maurice before you go to bed," she said.

"Thank you," I smiled at her and took the stairs two at a time.

I called Sylvia from my room.

"Edward?"

She'd caught the phone on the very first ring.

"Yes."

"Thank you for calling back," she said. "I hope you don't think I'm being foolish."

"About what?"

"About the manuscript."

I waited.

"Are you still there?" she asked.

"Yes. What about the manuscript, Sylvia?"

"It sounds so silly," she said. "But there's something Peter didn't tell you."

I waited some more.

"When he spoke to Maria the second time, when she cancelled the appointment?" She phrased it as a question.

"Yes?"

"Well, she said she thought the manuscript was cursed."

"Cursed?"

"That's exactly the word she used. She said she thought it might be cursed because of all the bad luck they'd been having since they found it."

"What bad luck?"

"Well, her son got sick the first time, and Eric broke his leg. Then her son got sick again. And there was more. She was quite serious. Peter told her she was being silly, told her there was no such thing as a curse."

"But you think there is?"

"I think there might be."

I was tired. My head ached. I needed to crawl into bed and damn the bedbugs.

"Okay," I said. "I'll make a note of it."

"Don't patronize me." She spoke sharply.

"I'm not patronizing you," I told her. "I just happen to agree with Peter. I don't believe in curses, Sylvia. Or witchcraft or satanic verses or little green men. Besides, I think Maria Glossard was forgetting something."

She waited before asking.

"Forgetting what?"

"The fact that you and Peter were paying her six thousand dollars for something that could turn out to be worthless." I paused. "I think that was a stroke of good luck," I said. "Don't you?"

I could hear her breathing on the other end of the phone.

"Good night, Edward."

She hung up before I could wish her the same.

Chapter Six

I SLEPT LIKE A BABY and woke later that morning, around ten o'clock. By which time, I'd missed breakfast. The dining room was closed until lunch.

"We only serve breakfast up to nine o'clock," the rosy-cheeked receptionist told me.

"Room service?" I asked.

"Certainly. What would you like?"

"Breakfast?"

"Right-oh."

So I had eggs and bacon with toast and marmalade in my room instead of downstairs. After breakfast and a lukewarm shower, I battled the British telephone system to find that the Glossards had an unlisted number.

Which meant I wasn't getting it, no matter how charming British Telecom thought I was.

What I needed, besides a gun, was a new cell phone. I asked Rosy-Cheeks where I might get one but she had no idea what I was talking about.

"A cell what, sir?" she repeated.

"A cell phone," I replied.

"What's one of them, then?"

"It's like a cordless only smaller. And you can take it with you wherever you go."

"Oh!" The penny finally dropped, as the Brits would say. "You mean a mobile!"

"A mobile? Is that like a phone?"

"Yes." She seemed excited, as if she'd won a game show. "Like this." She dug through her handbag and produced a lime green cell phone. "You can get one at the phone shop in St. Peter's Street."

"The main drag?" I asked and hastily rephrased the question. "The high street?"

"Yes." She pointed. "Turn left and it's halfway down on the left-hand side, just before the roundabout."

And indeed it was.

They wanted three pieces of ID before they let me have my own phone. I bought the prepaid option that gave me fifty pounds of airtime. About a hundred bucks worth. I declined the lime green model in favour of a black one with blue backlighting.

"What ring tone d'you want, then?" the bored young salesman asked.

"What have you got?"

He rattled off a few thousand options. I chose the Stones' "Start Me Up," which he said was a good choice. I got the impression he would have said the same thing if I'd asked for Handel's "Water Music." I wondered how much of my fifty quid went to the Glimmer Twins for using their song. I bought a belt holder too, so I could wear the phone on my hip.

Like a gun.

In a pinch, I could speed-dial the bad guys to death.

I considered renting a car to get to Crawley but thought better of it. Remembering to drive on the wrong side of the road seemed like too much work on my first full day. I could take the train into London, then take the subway, or the tube, as they called it, to south London, then take a taxi to the Glossard place from there. But the subway system required a guide, fluent in five languages, and a Global Positioning System that worked underground.

The heck with it, then.

I took a taxi from the hotel all the way to Crawley.

It was only money after all, and the good doctor needed a quick result.

I found a cheery Brit to do the driving. He called me "guv" and we agreed on a flat fee rather than the meter. I climbed in the back of his taxi and slid around on the polished leather like I was on a carnival ride. It was a real London taxi, the sort you see in the movies. Black, with room for just the driver up front. His name was Ronnie and he kept up a merry banter most of the way to Crawley.

"Don't tell me what you do for a living," he said. "I'm a bit psychic about stuff like that."

"All right." I played along, a little bored.

He adjusted the mirror so he could see me.

"If you're so psychic, how come you need to see me to figure out what I do for a living?"

"I knew you was gonna say that," he said and laughed. "D'you get it?"

"Unfortunately."

He angled the mirror on the traffic where it belonged.

"Right. I've got a plane in mind," he said. "But I think you just got off of one. I don't think you're a pilot or anything like that."

"Right."

"No, don't say anything," he said. "Lemme guess, all right?"

"All right."

He concentrated on his driving for a while then started up again.

"Yours isn't a regular job," he said. "Not one with regular hours. You're not a nine-to-fiver, that's for sure."

I remained impressively silent in the back.

"And you work for yourself," he said. "Contract like. People hire you, am I right?"

I didn't answer.

"Well?"

"You said not to say anything," I reminded him.

"Well, I weren't being literal," he said. "Am I right?"

"Not even close," I said. "I'm a gynecologist. I go around spreading old wives' tales."

He had a wonderful laugh. It was very infectious.

"You could be a stand-up comedian," he said, wiping a tear. "But that ain't it. I'll get it, hang about."

I slid around in the back as Ronnie steered hard around a traffic island. He didn't say anything for a while.

The closer we got to London, the more surveillance cameras I noticed. They were everywhere. On the tops of buildings, on poles, at almost every set of traffic lights. I hadn't noticed them on the way from the airport, but then I was tired and it was dark. I mentioned them to Ronnie.

"There's over two million of them now," he said. "Can't take a piss without someone watching you these days. But it keeps the nasty bastards off the streets, so it can't be all bad."

"Didn't do much keeping that serial killer off the streets though, did they?"

He looked over his shoulder at me, a quick head turn, then back to the road ahead.

"I got it," he said. "You're like a lawyer. No, no you're not. But you sometimes work for lawyers. Freelance. Helping them out. Like an investigator. That's it. You're an investigator. Like maybe a fire investigator. Or one of them insurance investigators. But you're private, working for yourself."

Son of a gun.

"I'll throw in another twenty if you tell me when I'm going to win the lottery."

"Save your money, guv," he said. "You'll always be a working stiff."

"I'm impressed," I said. "I'm an insurance adjuster. On vacation. So tell me, how'd you do it?"

"Dunno." He shrugged. "I've done it for years. Just for fun, mind. I'm right about eight out of ten times. Even been on the telly a few times, I have."

"Who was your toughest one?"

He thought for a moment.

"A mime," he said. "A big Aussie bastard. Picked him up outside a boozer one morning. Took him all the way to Watford before I guessed him. And he never said a word."

"Mimes don't," I said.

"You smart arse," he said but he chuckled.

As we drove through London, the conversation touched on Peter Maurice and "the 'orrible way that Yankee quack doctor killed them women." I didn't have the heart to tell him Peter was Canadian, nor that I was working for the accused.

If he was that good, he'd figure it out by himself.

We pulled over when we reached the outskirts of Crawley, and Ronnie checked his map, a battered old copy of London's A to Z.

"Right-oh, guv," he said. "I found it."

Cabbies call everyone guv, which is short for governor. I didn't let it go to my head.

We drove to Eric Glossard's house. It was at the far end of a short cul-de-sac, an ancient row of terraced houses on one side and a fenced-off, abandoned railway line on the other. The rain made it more depressing than it really was.

Or maybe not.

"I'll need you to wait," I told Ronnie.

I gave him my Visa card and signed for the return trip plus a sizable tip to make him feel even better about me.

"Ta very much," he said. "How long will you be, anyway, guv?"

"If the guy I'm looking for is home, maybe an hour."

"Mind if I go do a bit of shopping, then?"

I figured if he were going to spend my tip, he'd need at least an hour.

"Let me see if he's home first."

I crossed the cobblestoned street, slick with rain, and

knocked on Eric Glossard's door. It was painted a bright yellow, the only warm thing on the entire street. I heard somebody moving about inside, then a lock turned and the door opened three inches, held in place by a chrome security chain. A man with a pale, narrow face peered out.

"Yeah?"

"Eric Glossard?"

"Yeah?"

"I'm Eddie Dancer. I came all the way from Canada to talk with you."

"Yeah? Well, you can fuck off back to Canada. I ain't got nothin' to talk to you about."

He tried to slam the door but my foot was already in the gap.

"I'm willing to pay you for your time," I said, reasonably.

"Git yer fuckin' foot outta my door or lose it."

"Did you murder your wife, Eric? Is that why you don't want to talk to me?"

He looked incredulous. I took my foot away and the door slammed shut. The chain rattled, and the door flew open again. He would have launched himself at me if his leg weren't still in a cast.

"I'll fuckin' have you, so help me! I'll fuckin' kill you!"

The front room curtains next door flickered open and an old face pressed up against the glass.

I moved in close to Eric's open door.

"Eric. I'm here to help. Let me in. Make us a cup of tea, there's a good lad."

When he tried to grab my throat, I turned sideways and

hit him in the solar plexus with my elbow. I saw Ronnie watching.

"Come back in an hour!" I waved cheerfully.

Ronnie nodded.

"Right-oh, guv!"

He gunned the taxi in a tight circle and drove off down the cul-de-sac.

I pushed Eric gently backwards and stepped inside, closing the door behind me. I left my shoes on the mat, polite Canadian that I am, and helped Eric into a nearby chair. He was a tall, thin man and his jeans hung loosely as though he'd recently lost even more weight. He wore a heavy green sweater over a black turtleneck. His face was cratered with acne scars and he was missing a tooth.

He rubbed his stomach.

"That fuckin' 'urt, that did."

"I know."

"I could 'ave you for assault," he told me.

"You probably could," I agreed, "except I have a witness that you tried to grab me by the throat. And you threatened to kill me."

"What witness? A fuckin' cabbie?"

"Yes, but he's my fuckin' cabbie. And I tipped him very well."

Sullen, he glared at me.

"Look," I said, trying to be reasonable. "I could have broken your leg."

"S'already broken."

"Your other leg."

"Says who?" But his bravado was slipping.

"Eric." I looked at him. "It's a long way from Canada. How about that cup of tea?"

"Go to 'ell."

I watched him for a few moments, sitting there trying to get his breath back.

"Did you love her?"

"None of your fuckin' business."

"I'm sorry for your loss, Eric. I really am."

"You're the same as him. That Dr. Maurice. He's from Canada."

"I work for him."

He looked at me, still rubbing his stomach.

"That figures."

"He didn't do it, Eric."

"That's what they all say."

"And if he didn't, who did?"

"You think I killed my wife? And my kid?"

His eyes were rimmed red.

"Not for a minute," I told him.

"You said I did."

"I *asked* you if you did. There's a big difference."

"I need to talk to my lawyer. I ain't telling you nuffink."

"Call him." I stood back, folded my arms.

"I can't remember his number."

"How are you managing? Broken leg, no work. I know money's tight. Maria said so in her letter."

"What letter?" Interested now.

"The one she wrote to Dr. Maurice."

"I never read it."

I pulled out the copy, handed it to him.

"Go ahead."

I watched his face as he read the words from his dead wife. He was willing himself not to cry.

"Christ." He wiped his eyes but the tears wouldn't stop. "I can't read this. Not now." He took a troubled breath, his eyes full.

"Let it out, Eric," I said, quietly.

It was all he needed to hear. He crumpled the letter and his head dropped forward, shoulders trembling under the onslaught. I wondered if he'd cried this hard since he took the news. Wife and baby, both dead, both murdered, and here he was, living alone in the house where they'd died. I squatted down beside him, laid a hand on his shoulder and felt the heat of his pain through his thin, fragile frame.

He sobbed hard for a long time. I stayed next to him, rubbing his neck and shoulders until he was all sobbed out. His face was a mess, his nose all runny. You could see his ears, hot and red behind strands of long, thin hair.

I found a roll of toilet paper in the tiny downstairs bathroom and handed it to him. He honked and coughed and wiped his tears.

"Ta," he said when he was all spent.

"I'm here to help you, Eric."

"I wish," he said.

"I'm a private detective," I said. "Dr. Maurice hired me to find out who really killed those people."

"Why you? You ain't even from around 'ere."

"I'm good, though."

"You'd betta be."

"How about that cup of tea?" I asked.

"Yeah, all right." He sounded resigned now. He gathered himself and I helped him to his feet.

"Sorry about the elbow," I told him.

And I was.

"Ah." He waved it off. "Didn't 'urt that much," he said, putting on a brave face.

When he'd made the tea, we sat in the spotless kitchen and drank it together, like old mates. It was strong and sweet and it tasted good. Eric finished his before me and put his cup in the sink. He stood staring out the window for a long time before he spoke again.

"She died just there." He pointed to the floor behind him.

"I'm sorry. I had no idea."

"He came in through this window. He has this thing he carries with him. Plod says it's like a big nutcracker."

"Who's Plod?"

He looked at me for a moment.

"Plod. The police."

"Ah." I'd never heard them called that before.

"They say he must have assembled it when he got here. Must be five feet long, like two pair of ladders. He clamps it around their heads, and then walks up it. It's his weight and the length of the handles, see? It crushes their heads, caves them in. Reckoned it took twenty, maybe thirty minutes to kill her. It must have been agony. He raped her first. Upstairs. Evan was probably crying. He put my little boy between our mattresses, then raped Maria on top. Forced all the life outta my little boy. Suffocated him. Crushed him to death."

God almighty. Eric, you poor bastard. He was staring off into space. The thousand-yard stare. I wondered if he was on medication.

"Have you talked to anyone? A doctor? A shrink?"

He shook his head.

"Can't afford it."

Jesus H. Christ.

"What did this have to do with the manuscript?"

He shrugged.

"Dunno."

"Have you read it?"

He shook his head, slowly.

"It's all in Italian."

"Maria sent it to Dr. Maurice?"

He nodded.

"She was gonna send him the copy but, when the cheque cleared, she sent him the original."

I looked at him.

"You have a copy?"

He nodded silently.

"Is it here, in the house?"

He nodded.

"Upstairs."

"Could I see it?"

"You read Italian? Old Italian?"

"No."

"What's the point?"

"Can I see it anyway?"

He sighed, nodded again.

"I'll get it," he said.

He moved slowly, and it was painful to watch him maneuver up the stairs. While he was gone, I made a note of his phone number, in case I needed to call on him again. I rinsed the tea things in the sink and stacked them on the draining board before I heard him coming down the stairs, sideways, holding the rail for support.

He was carrying a green, three-ring binder.

"Here," he said, handing it to me at the bottom of the stairs.

I took it reverently. Thirty pages of photocopied manuscript. The pages had a dull grey hue and I visualized the original brown parchment paper. The handwriting was neat and spidery. Franz-Anton Mesmer's name underlined on the title page. I flipped though it, but it meant nothing to me.

"Is this for sale?"

He shrugged.

"I'll buy it from you. I'll make another copy and give you this one back. And I'll pay you the balance that Dr. Maurice owes you."

He looked at me.

"Won't bring them back though, will it?"

"No. But it might help me find the man who did it. And you could use the money."

He looked at me from behind a lifetime of hurt.

"All right." He nodded. "It's yours."

"I'll be back for it. I don't have any English money. I need to find a bank."

"Just take it," he said. "It's been nowt but fuckin' trouble since I found it. Maria thought it were cursed." He looked at me. "I think she might be right," he said.

"Did you make this copy?" I asked him.

"No. Maria did."

"Whereabouts?"

He shrugged, shook his head like he didn't know and couldn't care less.

I nodded. We shook hands. I gave him Peter Maurice's cheque for fifteen hundred pounds. He stared at it, then quickly put it away in his pocket.

"No charge." He nodded at the binder. "Paid in full."

"All right. Thanks. I'll see myself out," I told him, "and I'll bring this back in an hour."

"Don't even bovver," he said.

I sat on the doorstep while it threatened to rain again, waiting for Ronnie to come and pick me up. While I waited, I examined the binder. I found a price sticker. Maria had paid one pound twenty for the binder. The sticker read: *Office Copy and Supply. Crawley.*

When Ronnie arrived, there were parcels stacked on the seat.

"Just shove that lot out the way, guv." He looked over his shoulder as I climbed in. "Where now?" he said.

"Place called Office Copy and Supply."

"In Crawley?"

"Yes."

"Right, guv."

He made a tight turn and the parcels slid onto my lap. I pushed them away. Outside, I noticed rows of curtains moving to keep pace with us.

Nosy bleedin' neighbours.

Or maybe they were just looking out for one of their own.

Ronnie got on the radio and asked dispatch for the address of the store. The radio crackled something incomprehensible.

"Ta," Ronnie said. He glanced over his shoulder. "It's up a side street, not far. Them parcels in your way?"

"Nope."

I pushed them back again.

I was the perfect passenger, easygoing and a big tipper.

Chapter Seven

TUCKED AWAY UP A side street, as Ronnie said, was Office Copy and Supply. It was a cross between an office and a shop with a long counter at the far end. They had a variety of copiers, black-and-white and colour, and shelves of paper, pens and art supplies. A beautiful young girl, of Caribbean colour and descent, named-tagged Leah, came out from behind the counter to help me. I gave her the binder and tried not to stare at her long brown, slender legs as she bent over and unsnapped the pages from the binder, placed them face up on the feed tray and hit the start button.

"You're American, aren't you? I love your accent," she said, in that marvelous singsong voice of the Islands. She made me think of steel drums and brilliant white beaches, palm trees and naughty thoughts.

"Canadian," I said and she gave me an even warmer smile. Much warmer, I thought, than any American would ever get. She three-hole punched the pages she had copied for me and found a matching green binder.

I thanked her and she told me I was "very much welcome." Our hands touched as she handed me my change across the counter.

I think she was flirting.

When we got to Eric's house in the cul-de-sac, he wouldn't answer the door. I could hear him inside, crying. The binder wouldn't fit through the mailbox in his front door. I thought about feeding the pages individually through the mail slot but decided that was probably a bad idea.

I had no choice but to keep both copies.

Maybe it was best that way.

I called his house from my cell phone as I stood outside. He didn't pick up, but then I didn't expect he would. I left him a brief message, including my mobile phone number, just in case, and hung up.

"Where now, guv?" Ronnie asked.

I moved the recalcitrant parcels to the far side of the long seat.

"Home, James," I said. "And don't spare the horses."

"Right, guv."

He swung the taxi around and his parcels fell on me like an avalanche. I moved them across the seat and settled down for the long ride home.

A few minutes later, an odd thing happened.

Ronnie became agitated.

He turned off the main road onto a side street and stopped his cab. He didn't turn to look at me, just angled his driving mirror in my direction.

And there was something in his eyes that bothered me.

"Them things," he said. "I wan' 'em locked in the boot."

His tone was serious.

"What things?" I asked, cautiously.

"Them."

I held up the binders.

"These?"

He nodded.

"Yeah, them."

He looked anxious. I would have pursued it but the look in his eyes suggested I shouldn't. I shrugged and did as he asked. When I got back inside the cab, he sat for a few seconds without saying anything.

He finally turned in my direction.

"It's not always fun," he said. "Sometimes I get really bad feelings about things. Like them binders. I don't know what's in 'em and, God knows, I don't wanna know." He held my eye. "And believe me, guv, neither do you."

I nodded to acknowledge his concern.

He pulled away from the curb without another word and drove sedately all the way to St. Albans.

As I told Sylvia, I don't believe in curses or witchcraft or any of that silly psychic nonsense.

But maybe I should buy a rabbit's foot.

It probably couldn't hurt.

Yeah.

Tell that to the rabbit.

Chapter Eight

IT WAS SUPPERTIME when Ronnie dropped me at the Queens Hotel. The rosy-faced receptionist told me that my belongings had been sent to the Maurices' house. She was quite frosty and I guessed she had learned the Tabloid Truth about Peter Maurice.

She wasn't too upset to take his money though.

I walked down the hill to the Maurices' house, now my home for the duration of my stay in England. The street was narrow, winding past rows of high-end shops full of shoes and furs and watches and wine. When the shops ended, I got a real surprise. To my left was the overpowering majesty of St. Albans Cathedral, an immense and beautiful structure towering above me in the fading light. I'd had no idea it was there. I'd walked right past it in the wee small hours, my head angled against the rain. I stood and stared at the huge structure. You didn't need to be a history buff to be impressed by its size or its age. I read a plaque that told of the discovery of Roman remains dating back almost a thousand years, when the Romans came to conquer.

A thousand years ago?

Canada was still an iceberg.

Despite the cold, the walk was pleasant. As I approached the house, I saw a small collection of cars and SUVs cluttering the road. Men stood around in a small, intimate group. I recognized the motorcyclist among them from the night before.

They were the paparazzi.

I pulled the ski mask from inside my coat and wiggled it down over my ears. The paparazzi were on me thirty feet from the gate.

There was a concerted mad rush towards me. Cameras whirred and clicked. Flashbulbs burned my eye bulbs. But that's all they got. The ski mask concealed my face and they pleaded with me to take it off.

I ignored them and unlatched the wooden gate. I walked to the front door and the paparazzi stayed behind on the sidewalk. A different policeman stood on duty. I wondered why they needed him, since Peter was in custody. I rolled the ski mask off my face.

"Good evening, sir." He touched his forelock.

"Good evening, Plod."

He looked a bit miffed. Maybe Plod lacked the air of affection I intended. I rang the doorbell.

"I live here now," I told him.

"I believe the door's unlocked, sir," Plod said, a little stiffly.

I tried the handle and the door opened ahead of me. I stepped inside, thanked him and closed it behind me, then kicked off my shoes.

"Sylvia? Hello?"

She was in the kitchen, sipping tea. A large, elderly man in a three-piece pinstriped suit and a red-and-black tie sat next to her.

"Edward." Sylvia stood up and air kissed my cheek. "Edward, this is Geoffrey Lansdale, our solicitor."

He looked me over before standing, making it an effort to push his large frame out of the chair. We shook hands. It was like clapping your hand around a dead fish. The skin on his face and neck was gathered like an old bulldog's with pale, overlapping creases, and his eyes were baggy, the whites yellowed like his teeth. His graying moustache curled down over his top lip and crept into his mouth.

"Pleasure," he said, without much pleasure.

"Charmed," I said, without much charm.

It was obvious we didn't take to one another. We stared like old adversaries, and it went downhill from there.

"So," I said. "Where's Peter?"

"In a St. Albans police cell, I imagine," he said.

"You imagine?" I said.

"He's in prison," he said, firmly.

"Can't you get him out?"

"I'm trying."

"Try harder."

"Mr. Dancer," he said testily, "I'm really not sure of your role in any of this."

"I'm the hired gun," I said. "I shoot people when things get out of hand."

"And whom have you shot so far?"

"Early days," I replied, and I gave him my nasty smile.

"Well, I'm working to effect Dr. Maurice's release," he said. "I trust your being here isn't going to affect my efforts."

"Have you effected the release of the manuscript yet?" I asked him.

"Of course not," he said, primly. "It's not likely to be released. It's evidence."

"Present for you." I dropped a copy of the bound manuscript on the kitchen counter.

"What's this?" he asked, warily.

"The manuscript. Or, to be more precise —" I mimicked his overbearing style "— a copy thereof."

"Where did you get this?" He spoke sharply.

"Do you want it or not?"

"I want to know where you got it."

"Eric Glossard gave it to me."

He blinked big eyes, like an owl considering its dinner.

"You've spoken with Eric Glossard?" Like he didn't believe me.

"We took tea together this afternoon."

"Sylvia." He looked to Peter's wife for help. "I'm not sure this is helping Peter's case one iota."

"Really? I thought Edward did rather well, considering," she said.

"Mrs. Maurice." He straightened his tie. "You need to consider who is running Peter's defence, my dear lady."

She bristled.

This was fun.

"Consider?" she said. "Or reconsider?"

He was taken aback.

"Now see here," he spluttered.

"No, Geoffrey, I won't be browbeaten. Edward is a private detective. And a very good one. My husband needs all the help he can get. If you're uncomfortable with Edward's involvement, get over it. Or get out."

She stood her ground and I kept shtum. Finally, Geoffrey picked up the binder from the kitchen counter.

"I'll review this," was all he said.

"It's Old Italian," I reminded him.

"So's my wife," he said, and I detected a certain smugness. "Gina was born in Italy in nineteen thirty-six. Is that old enough?"

"I want to meet her," I told him. "Tomorrow morning."

"We'll see."

He retrieved his overcoat from the chair and left rather rudely without saying good night.

"You can keep that copy!" I called to him down the hall. "I have another!" When he still didn't respond, I childishly called after him again. "You're welcome!"

"Thank you!" he barked, finally, before slamming the front door behind him.

"He's what the Brits call a pompous old fart, I'm afraid," Sylvia said, "but he's the only pompous old fart we've got."

"Let's hope he's all we need," I replied.

She came over and stood in front of me, close enough to rest her head against my shoulder. Instinctively, I put my hand against her back, feeling the warmth of her skin through my palm, setting fire to my fingertips. She was taking this hard. She needed some reassurance.

"Rough day, eh?" I said.

"Yes." She spoke softly.

"Did you go with him?"

"They wouldn't let me."

I felt the heat of her breath caress my neck.

As we stood there, I became aware of a movement in the back garden beyond the kitchen window.

A sudden flash lit up the kitchen.

"Ah, Christ!"

I was out the kitchen door before he knew it. When he saw me, he turned to run. I was two steps behind him as he raced down the brick walkway towards the high wall that bordered the property. I timed it perfectly and as he came down on his right foot, I clipped the outside of his left foot, just enough to throw it off balance. It hooked behind his right ankle and he went flying, his camera bouncing off the brickwork ahead of him. I stepped on him in stocking feet, driving him hard into the footpath, winding him, and I grabbed the camera before he could recover. I swung it hard by the strap, slamming it into the brickwork. It shattered into a dozen pieces.

"Shit!" he gasped and rolled upright. "That's a really —" he took a breath "— expensive camera!"

"Not anymore."

"What's all this, then?"

It was Plod, coming around from the front.

"Thought you were supposed to keep out the riff-raff?" I said.

"He must have climbed over the wall," Plod said in disbelief, as if the six-foot wall would keep out an army.

"No shit, Sherlock." I noticed my feet were cold. "If he comes back again, charge him with trespass."

I walked inside and locked the door behind me.

"Edward?"

She hadn't moved.

"Paparazzi," I said. "Maybe we should keep all the drapes closed for the next few days."

"Yes, of course. I'm sorry." She looked worried.

"Nothing to be sorry about," I said.

We sat in the kitchen after that. We drank our way through a bottle of wine and, later, ate supper together, moving to the drawing room to finish our coffee. Once I'd settled into the plush upholstery, I realized just how tired I was. I tried to be polite but it was hard to keep my eyes open. She took the cup and saucer from my hand and placed them on the side table.

"I'll run you a bath," she said. "Then you should really get some sleep."

She'd added scented bath salts to the water and I slid down the bathtub and let the heat of the water untangle the knots of the last day and a half. When the water cooled, I topped it up from the hot tap and stayed in until my fingers turned prune-like.

My bedroom was at the back of the house. As I passed the head of the stairs, I called down to wish Sylvia good night but I think she was watching television and didn't hear me.

Or maybe she had dozed off.

I climbed into bed and snuggled beneath a mountain of blankets, letting the pillows take the weight off my neck. Alone in bed, waiting for sleep to overtake me, I tried very hard not to think about Eric Glossard's little boy trapped between the mattress and box spring of his mother's bed while the monster slowly crushed the life from his fragile little boy's body.

Before I fell asleep, I let God know that I would not let that particular sin go unpunished.

Chapter Nine

IT BEGAN TO RAIN AGAIN just before dawn. Hard and foul and fuelled by powerful winds from the north. The heavy rain raked across the roof tiles and pebbled the window, streaking the glass with unbroken strings of ice water. The wind made the house creak, and I was cold even beneath the blankets. It wasn't a warm, moist chinook breeze but a vicious wind from the cold North Sea. A biting wind, baying against the brickwork like a pack of hounds out for blood.

The house itself was quite nice, maybe even imposing, and, while I'm no architectural whiz, I could recognize the Tudor influence. But it had been built more than a hundred years ago, long before the advent of central heating.

The whole place was like a giant ice cube.

And I needed to get out of bed to make a phone call.

I stared at the ceiling for several minutes, willing myself to brave the elements before I mustered the courage to throw back the covers, jump out of bed, run across the room, grab my mobile phone off the dresser and dive back under the covers, all while shivering alarmingly. When I warmed up half a degree, half an hour later, I dialed Cindy Palmer's number in Calgary, eight thousand miles away.

"Hello?" She answered on the third ring.

"The Queen says hi."

"Which one?"

"Of England."

There was a pause.

"I thought you were joking," she said.

"I wish. It's colder than the Arctic, pouring with rain, and I'm alone in a bed made lonelier by your absence."

"Absence makes the heart grow fonder."

"This is true, but it doesn't do much for the libido."

"You could take something for that," she said.

"Yeah. Bromide."

We talked for twenty minutes and she never once asked me why I was in England. It's not that she doesn't care or that my life's work bores her silly. It's because she knows my work can sometimes be dangerous. And she prefers not to be reminded of that fact. As an emergency-room nurse, she sees the results of dangerous occupations on a daily basis. Her ex-husband was a cop and she has an eleven-year-old daughter whom she needs to protect and cherish and who had already experienced the dark side of my darker life.

"Do you remember Dr. Maurice?" I asked her finally. "Peter Maurice?"

"Yes," she said, rather flatly I thought, but that could have been the phone line.

"He's on a book tour over here. He's been accused of multiple murders."

"Really," she said.

"Yes."

"That's why you're in England?"

"Yes."

"Well." She paused before adding, "He's in very good hands, then."

"Thank you."

"I wish I were."

"Me, too," I said.

"Hurry home, Eddie."

"I will."

"Gotta go."

"Love to Lindsay," I said. Lindsay was her daughter. "And to Norman." Norman was her cat.

"I'll tell them," she promised. "Now, I've really got to go."

"So, go."

We listened to each other breathing for a while. We were like love-stricken teenyboppers. It was ridiculous but she filled my senses with her presence.

"Hang up," I told her.

"You first."

See?

Teenage angst.

I hung up the phone. Well, technically, I guess I pressed the Off button. We need some rules of disengagement. Whomsoever instigates the call shall ultimately be responsible for uninstigating it when the time comes.

The wind was blowing even harder. It moaned and screeched beneath and around the eaves and chased the rain across the tiles. Beyond the back of the house, it blew piles of soggy leaves through a forest of trees. I remembered reading once that it rains every day somewhere in the United Kingdom.

That's a good enough reason not to unite.

Chapter Ten

AFTER MY MORNING SHIVER, shave and shower, I dressed in layers to ward off the dampness. The smell of roasted toast and perked coffee drew me downstairs to the kitchen where Sylvia sat staring at the morning paper.

"Good morning." I tried a smile but her face was a mask. "What's up?" I asked and she turned the newspaper around.

We'd made the front page of the tabloids.

I thought the paparazzi used 35mm film. Obviously, our intruder was using digital and my efforts to reduce his equipment to rubble hadn't damaged the memory card. The headline read *CONSOLATION PRIZE?* Beneath it was a photograph of Sylvia leaning on my shoulder. You could just make out the back of my head. The story detailed Peter's arrest and speculated on the identity of the man consoling Peter's "lovely and vivacious wife."

"Not my best side," I said and pushed the paper across the table. "Have you thought about returning to Canada?"

"By myself?"

"Yes. This sort of stuff —" I tapped the paper "— will only get worse."

"Oh, it already has."

She stood and beckoned me to follow. In the master bedroom, she moved the drapes a quarter inch. I stood close to her and looked out. The crowd of paparazzi had grown to maybe thirty or forty people. All men. They crowded the sidewalk around the entrance gate, carrying cameras protected beneath layers of plastic. Many more cars and SUVs were lined up across the street and most had their engines running.

"They arrived sometime after midnight," she said and I realized she hadn't had much sleep.

"Why don't we find somewhere more private for you? I can make a few calls, find someplace out of the way."

She shook her head.

"No. I want to be close to Peter. Besides, I'll be visiting him every day. There's no way I can outrun them. They can smell a story a mile away."

"The joys of free enterprise," I said.

"I want to see Peter today," she said. "This morning. Will you come with me?"

"Soon as I grab some breakfast," I said.

"Of course." She shook her head as though she realized she had forgotten her manners. "I'll make some for you."

She made me scrambled eggs with thick buttered toast and marmalade on the side while I read the morning paper. Domestic bliss. I almost put my feet up. She poured me a large mug of coffee and stirred in a spoonful of sugar and I let her wait on me hand and foot, but only because it took her mind off everything else that was going on and not because I'm part male chauvinistic pig.

Even though I thoroughly enjoyed it.

After breakfast, I phoned Geoffrey Lansdale at his office but it was too early for him. The answering service told me his office wouldn't open until ten. I found his home number and called him there.

"We're going to see Peter this morning," I told him without preamble. "Has your wife read the manuscript?"

"Hardly," he said, in a voice crustier than breakfast toast.

"When might she?"

"Later today."

"When can I meet with her?"

"You seem to have the home phone number," he bristled. "Call her this afternoon."

"Can you meet us at the police station?"

"Not until ten-thirty." He remained curt.

"Give me directions, then."

He told me the best route to take from the house. It wasn't too far.

"Do you have a cell?" I asked him.

"A what?"

"A mobile phone?"

"Yes."

"Give me your number."

He hesitated. When he gave it to me, he warned me it was for emergencies only.

I hung up mid-warning.

"You still have a car?" I asked Sylvia.

"Yes," she said. "There's no overnight parking outside.

Unless you're the paparazzi, then you can park wherever you like. We're in a parking lot down the street."

"We can probably lose them," I told her. "But they'll have the police station staked out. Let's play it by ear. I'll get the car and pull up close to the gate." I realised I'd be sitting on the right-hand side of the car, blocking her. "You'll have to climb in the back," I said.

"Won't they follow you when you leave the house?"

"Only if they see me leave," I said.

I went out the back way and over the same wall the snoopy reporter had used the night before. The wall was thick with spongy moss and the ground was soggy underfoot. I left a nice set of footprints in the grass. There was a narrow band of trees behind the property, then a strip of green space. From my bedroom window, I had seen a small lake in the distance, fed by a fat stream of black, sluggish water that flowed around the back of the property. The stream curled in towards the back wall, then curled away again. The thicket of trees gave good cover.

But not that good.

I saw both figures moving quickly towards me through the trees as I jumped from the wall. They had built a makeshift shelter, a black tarp strung between the branches.

"Hey!" The larger of the two called me.

I ignored him and kept moving.

The other one took my picture with a telephoto lens but I didn't care, I was wearing the ski mask again. I recognized him from the night before. I'd smashed his camera in the back yard.

"Wait up!" the big one yelled as he hurried over.

They tried to block my path. The photographer raised his camera and fired off half a roll.

"Take that off," the heavier of the two said, pointing at the ski mask. "Give us a picture. Least you can do after smashing his camera."

I shook my head and waved them aside.

"I'll get it off," the bigger man said and came at me through the trees.

I turned sideways to him, bent at the knees. He slowed down as he came within arm's reach.

"Last chance." He sounded winded. "Get it off."

I remain silent, unknowable.

He looked at the photographer.

"Ready?" he said and the man with the camera nodded.

Then he stepped up to grab the ski mask. I knew my rights. Even in England. I had to let him touch me first. The moment the fingers of his right hand brushed the cloth of the balaclava, I grabbed his extended hand, stepped into him and twisted his hand backwards against the joint. I was at ninety degrees to him now. I pried him up on his toes and you could hear the tendons in his wrist and elbow creak in protest. I held him there for a moment, giving him the chance to back off. He misread my intent as a moment of weakness and tried to sledgehammer me in the head with his left fist. I ducked and the blow passed overhead. I switched my grip from his hand to his wrist and gave it more torque. He flailed backwards, off balance. I bent my right arm and swung around in a quarter circle, clipping his jaw with the point of my elbow.

He went down in a heap.

The man with the camera caught it all on film. When he used up the roll, he held the camera over his head, as if it were out of bounds.

He was on my right as I walked past him, as if to ignore him. Just when he thought he was safe, I turned fast, my left leg extended, scribing a semicircle in the air, catching him behind the knees. He was already a little off balance, and I swept his legs out from under him. He pitched backwards, dropping his hands to cushion the fall. For a split-second, the camera floated in mid-air.

It was all the time I needed.

I hit the camera squarely with the flat of my hand, sending it up and out in a high arc. The strap made a series of lazy loops against the dark gray sky.

A homer.

I moved ahead and heard the satisfying splash as the camera hit the flat, brackish water, where it sank without trace.

I heard the man yelling, but wisely, he chose not to follow. I shimmied over the wall a hundred yards farther south and dropped into the parking lot. There were nine cars parked there. Sylvia said hers was black. There were four black ones. I used the key and found Sylvia's car on the third try. It was parked next to an orange-and-green van.

What the Brits call a Shagging Wagon.

Sylvia was watching from the master bedroom as I squeezed through the throng of paparazzi. I mounted the sidewalk, nearly taking out another photographer, who banged on the roof and stuck up two fingers at me.

The Brits' equivalent of flipping me the bird.

I parked so close to the gate, there wasn't enough room for a mouse to squeeze through. The moment they realized I was picking up Sylvia, they began taking pictures. Flashbulbs popped but all they saw of me were the whites of my eyes.

I could imagine the headlines:

MASKED MYSTERY MAN WHISKS AWAY WIFE

I unlocked the back door just as Sylvia reached the car, then I gunned it back onto the road as soon as she climbed in. I almost ran over one of our nosier neighbours, an elderly woman in a red housecoat, brandishing an umbrella as though it were a sword.

"Left!" Sylvia screamed. "They drive on the left!"

Damned Brits! Why couldn't they drive on the right like the rest of us? I swerved around the astonished woman, who seemed transfixed by the scene before her.

Horns honked, engines raced and the paparazzi, in full flight, tore up the road behind us. I slowed down, driving close to the centre line to block them from passing. As we neared the top of the hill, the lone motorcycle shot through a gap and pulled in front of me. It was a BMW. A big, powerful bike with ABS brakes. I wouldn't want to ride in that weather without ABS either. The passenger was sitting backwards, like a tail gunner, aiming his camera at the car. His licence plate read *STIX*. Approaching a set of traffic lights, I flicked the left turn signal on and watched the photographer signal the driver to make the left turn. As he turned left at the lights directly ahead of me, I slowed to a crawl in the junction. When the lights turned red a few seconds later, I gunned the car sharp right, cutting in front of the oncoming traffic.

The entourage stalled behind us and I made a few quick lefts and rights, not really trying that hard to lose them, just enjoying myself. St. Albans looked to be a nice town, built around a hill that featured an ancient clock tower as its focal point. I managed to stay on the correct side of the road most of the way to the police station, though it was getting unbearably hot beneath the ski mask.

I probably wouldn't need it much longer.

The paparazzi would find out who I was soon enough.

It's what they are good at.

But why make their job any easier?

Chapter Eleven

WE PARKED IN THE POLICE station visitors' parking lot. Most of the paparazzi had guessed where we were headed and were waiting for us when we arrived. We battled our way up the steps and into the station. It was a big building, long and low like a glass brick. The press poured in around us, yelling questions and firing off another barrage of flashbulbs until an irate desk sergeant bellowed at them to "keep the bloody racket down!" When that didn't work, he came out from behind the reception counter and gave all those who weren't there on official police business exactly five seconds to: "Get the hell out or get booked for obstruction!" Given his height and poundage, they moved quickly outside.

"You!" He glared at the ski mask. "Get that thing off your 'ead!"

"Just as soon as I'm out of camera range," I told him.

He didn't like it but he could see my point. He directed us to a door beyond the reception counter. It led into a corridor, shielded from the hordes outside.

"Now take it off!" he barked.

"Gladly."

I pulled the mask over my head. My hair was a fright but I don't think anyone cared.

"Are you Sylvia Maurice?" The sergeant ignored me.

"I am." She stood straight, her head held high. "We're here to see my husband."

"I know who you're here to see," he said, dripping sarcasm.

He turned and stared at me, waiting for me to tell him who I was. I stared back, waiting for him to put it in the form of a question. We stood like that for a while.

"Sergeant?" Sylvia broke the spell between us.

"Who's he?" the sergeant asked.

"He's working with my husband." She turned to me. "He's a private investigator."

"He can wait out here."

"No. I'm here to meet my client."

He stared at me some more.

"We do things differently over here," he said.

"Which explains your lousy reputation."

His cheeks flushed a deep red.

"You're not going anywhere," he declared.

Sylvia leaned in and read his nametag.

"Sergeant Roberts," she said. "I'm aware of our rights. We are both entitled to meet with my husband. If you continue to make my life any more difficult than it already is, I will go outside right now and hold a press conference on your station house steps. And believe me, you will be on the midday news."

Sergeant Roberts flinched. He knew she meant it. His face turned sour as he fought to control his anger.

"Down that corridor." He pointed the way. "They'll buzz you in. Someone will escort you to the interview room." He turned his back on us and stormed off.

People stared from the offices on either side as we walked the length of the corridor. The scarlet woman and her mysterious friend. I figured they didn't house multiple murderers there very often.

A police guard buzzed us in as promised. He called for a female officer and she took Sylvia into a separate room. The male guard searched me thoroughly. I assumed Sylvia was getting the same treatment. They kept my loose change and car keys, along with Sylvia's handbag, for safekeeping. If they hoped to find anything that would identify me in my wallet, they were disappointed.

We followed them both the short distance to the interview room.

There was a table and four chairs. The only thing on the table was a copy of today's paper with our photograph on the front page.

"How very classy," I said.

I rolled it up and jammed it hard under the male guard's arm. At least he had the decency to look embarrassed.

"You can sit this side," he said and waved us to our seats. "No touching. No passing anything back or forth. You'll be supervised at all times. Is that clear?"

"Peter Maurice is my husband," Sylvia said. "You can't expect me not to touch him."

"If you do, the interview's over. I don't make the rules, Mrs. Maurice, but I do enforce them. Now, is that clear?"

I touched her on the sleeve, guided her to a chair beside me.

"It's clear," I told him.

He waited a moment before stepping outside, leaving the female cop to guard us. I wasn't worried. I could take her in a pinch. When the other guard returned, he had Dr. Peter Maurice in tow. Peter was wearing his own clothes but they were rumpled, as if he'd slept in them. Which of course he had. His arms were handcuffed behind his back and he looked like he'd aged ten years. His hair was unkempt and there were dark circles beneath his eyes. Sylvia stood up, reached her hand towards him. It was a reflexive gesture, not designed to break the rules of engagement. I tugged her down and saw tears in the corner of her eye.

"Oh, Peter." She put her hand to her mouth. "I'm so sorry."

"I've had better days," Peter said, trying to lighten the mood. "Can you please loosen these?" he asked the policeman.

The man undid Peter's handcuffs and held the chair for him, then leaned against the door, trying for unobtrusive. The lady cop ducked out. She had more important things to do with her morning.

Like maybe her nails.

"Edward." Peter turned towards me. "Any progress?"

"A little," I said, inclining my head half a degree towards the officer pretending not to be listening. "I met a tourist from Meersburg. Big fan of Xerox. Geoff's wife is European, is she not? Maybe I'll have something concrete by four."

Short of talking in sign language, it was the best I could do to let Peter know that we had a copy of the manuscript and should have a translation later that afternoon.

"How are they treating you, Peter?" Sylvia looked concerned.

"About what I expected." He tried a smile. "The cells are small and very noisy. I missed a whole night's sleep, I'm afraid."

"Will they keep you here?" I asked.

"I don't know. These cells aren't designed for the long haul. Geoffrey's working to have me released into his custody but it all takes time."

"Who's the arresting officer?"

Peter looked at me and I could tell his mind had gone blank. He turned to the policeman leaning against the door.

"Detective Inspector Gerry Newcombe," the policeman said. Despite his feigned indifference, he was listening to our every word. "He's with Scotland Yard," he added. "He's going to move you to London in a day or two."

"It's so unfair," Sylvia said. "How could they even think that of you?" She rooted through her pocket for a tissue.

"Is there anything you need, Peter?" I asked, trying for practical.

"There's not much I'm allowed," he said. "Maybe a book. A writing pad and pencil would be nice."

"No pens or pencils." The policeman shook his head.

There was a firm knock on the door and the policeman pushed himself upright. He opened the door a crack and poked his head outside. I could hear people talking in the corridor.

"Your lawyer's here to see you, Dr. Maurice," the policeman said over his shoulder.

"Send him in, please."

"Can't, sir. You're only allowed two visitors at a time."

I stood up.

"I'll go," I said. I looked at Sylvia. "I may need the car. Lansdale can give you a ride back, if that's okay."

She shrugged. "I really don't need it, Edward. You take it."

I said goodbye to Peter. I could see he wanted to reach out, to shake me by the hand, but we both held back. I stepped outside. A different uniformed police officer walked me down the corridor to where Geoffrey Lansdale was waiting. He was looking pleased with himself.

"Oh, it's you," he said when he saw me.

"Sylvia's with Peter. Can you give her a ride home when you're done?"

"It's a bit inconvenient."

"That's not what I asked."

"Very well." He sighed like a martyr and began to move down the corridor.

"We're not done yet," I said. "What time can I see your wife?"

"This afternoon." He pulled a business card from his wallet and scribbled something on the back. "At four o'clock. No sooner. Here's the address." He handed me his card.

"One more thing." I handed him the ski mask. "Take this back to the house with you. Wear it if you want."

You'd think I'd handed him a bagful of dead rats.

Chapter Twelve

THE PAPARAZZI WERE hanging around like a pack of hyenas that'd missed lunch. I decided to leave Sylvia's car where it was and walk. I turned down the long corridor and found a door at the rear. It led out of the building through a concreted area where coppers who smoked did so in the rain. I walked past them, their shoulders hunched against the steady downpour as they sucked in damp cigarette smoke. I cut across a bank of wet grass and made a left turn when I reached the side street. I walked away quickly without breaking into a run. Nobody followed me. No motorbikes roared up behind me. Nobody took my picture.

I hiked through the town centre in the rain. I wore my made-in-Canada Far West waterproof jacket, so I stayed relatively dry as I looked for the Hertz Rent-a-Car office. I figured Sylvia's car would be a decoy and I'd rent a car for myself. How hard could it be, driving on the wrong side of the road?

Walking gave me a good perspective on the town. It was quaint and ancient, dating back hundreds of years. Tucked between various buildings were lots of narrow alleyways, barely wide enough for a car. I walked them all and found what I was looking for after an hour.

The Hertz office was overly bright and hotter than the inside of a toaster. The bright young thing behind the counter gave me her hundred-watt smile.

"Welcome to Hertz. How can we help you today?" She beamed at me, trying even harder.

"I need a car," I said, rather obviously. "Actually, I need two."

"Certainly," she said.

"One with a sunroof."

"Hmm." She looked thoughtful. "We've only got one with a sunroof. It's a Mercedes-Benz."

"Okay," I said. "But I don't need a Mercedes-Benz."

"But you need a sunroof," she said.

"Yes," I agreed. "But the rate for the Mercedes is probably double the rate for anything else."

"Do you have American Express?"

"I do."

"Good. We have a special promotion on at the moment," she said. "If you use your Amex card, you can get unlimited mileage or a free upgrade."

"I'll take the upgrade," I said, since I wasn't planning to put too many miles on it.

"But you want two?"

"The other can be anything," I said. "A compact, even."

"I've got a Fiat Seicento," she said. "It's yellow." She pulled a face and pointed to a four-wheeled block of aged cheese parked on the lot.

She offered me the Gorgonzola discount and I used my Amex card to pay for both cars.

"Who else will be driving?" she asked.

"I'm not sure," I said. "Can I call you?"

"Certainly." She beamed some more. It was all very jolly.

"I'll take the Mercedes now," I said. "Can you leave the cheese out front? I'll pick it up later in the week."

"We'll give it a good clean, sir," she said, trying even harder than before.

We walked around both cars in the rain to make sure there were no dings or dents unaccounted for. I initialed a few bits of paper and we shook hands. She handed me two sets of keys and wished me a safe and trouble-free visit to the British Isles.

She was a little late on that score.

The Mercedes was a four-door model. Pale blue with a sunroof that had probably never been opened. I made sure it worked then closed it and rummaged through the glovebox until I found the map of St. Albans she'd assured me was in there. I located Geoffrey Lansdale's street and drove the route. It took about fifteen minutes. Following the map again, I found my way to the public library. It was half a block up from the police station. I took a quick peek as I drove by the station. The paparazzi were still there, hanging like an L.A. street gang. I asked the gods to pour buckets on their intrusive and ungodly heads.

I pushed my way through the library's heavy door. The place was cavernous and my footsteps echoed loudly off the tiled floor. At the help desk, an overly friendly older lady, plump as a ripe peach with improbably blue hair, helped me find what I was looking for. She smelled of vanilla, and her fingernails, worn long, were painted gold with silver stars. She sat next to me and leaned over, resting her heavy bosom against my shoulder as I cranked the microfiche machine under her schoolmarmish guidance.

"There you go, luv." She patted the top of my thigh. "If you need anything else, anything at all, just come and get me. My name's Sandra."

"Thank you, Sandra." I moved her hand from my thigh to hers and patted it. It felt like a large and clammy lump of unbaked bread. "You've been a big help already."

"It's no trouble," she said. "I've always had a soft spot —" she put her unbaked hand back on my thigh "— for our Americans cousins."

"And we appreciate it," I said.

"Y'all come back, now," she said, eyelids all aflutter.

It was the worst attempt at a Southern accent I'd ever heard.

It took about an hour to find everything. I scoured the national papers, amazed how many there were for such a small country. I collected names, dates, times and places. Eleven murders, including the Glossards' son, Evan. Ten towns. I copied everything in order, from the first grisly find to the last.

Detective Inspector Gerry Newcombe picked up the case after the fourth murder. From then on, every crime scene was his. The media christened the killer "The Crusher." Eric Glossard wasn't exaggerating. The police believed the Crusher carried a portable contraption, like two pair of nutcrackers, ganged up side by side. Estimates varied but it was generally agreed the handles needed to be at least four or five feet long, since it required a force of more than a thousand pounds to crush a human skull. Someone had provided the thought-provoking comparison that it took merely six hundred pounds to crush a coconut.

Forensic evidence suggested most of the women, if not all, had died very slowly. One of the newspapers described, in minute detail with accompanying diagrams, the changes that a skull would go through under such intense pressure. As if we needed it spelled out how excruciatingly painful it was for those women who died. Seven of the ten women had been raped. Before he'd murdered them. It was assumed he'd run out of time to rape the other three.

I wondered how Eric Glossard slept at night.

There was all the extra coverage, too. Interviews with experts on human behaviour, sounding off on everything from motive to childhood trauma to modus operandi. Most of it was pure speculation, a lot of it drivel and some of it out-and-out fantasy.

There was one thing all the murders had in common, though.

Six of the murders had happened inside the women's homes, two in garages adjoining their homes and two at their places of work, after hours. In every single case, the killer had entered through a window, never through a door.

For some unknown reason, he had a very powerful aversion to going through doors. Or else a very strong attraction to going through windows.

When I finished with the present, it was time to delve

into the past. I folded my notes, tucked them away and moved to the bank of public access computers. The one I was on defaulted to the MSN web page and I typed in Franz-Anton Mesmer and let Google do its thing. It told me it had found 3,590 hits in just 0.29 seconds.

Like I cared.

I surfed the listings and read a lot about Mesmer that I had not known. He was born near Lake Constantine on May 23, 1734, and was the founder of something called Mesmerism, which I probably could have guessed. He obtained his doctorate from the University of Vienna in 1766. He travelled a lot after that, mainly around Europe, where he developed a system of healing based on his belief that all living beings contained a "magnetic fluid." By balancing this bodily fluid, he believed he could restore a patient's physical health. He called this force "animal gravity" but later changed it to "animal magnetism," probably because "animal gravity" wasn't confusing enough. It was probably no wackier than some of the claims coming out of the great state of California these days. In fact, Mesmer's theory probably made more sense.

To achieve this purported balance of bodily fluid, Mesmer designed something he called a *baquet,* which sounds a lot like a modern-day hot tub. It was an oval-shaped wooden tub filled with iron filings and something called "mesmerized water," which I hoped wasn't water that had passed through Mesmer before it hit the iron filings. Moveable iron rods protruded from the lid of the hot tub, and his patients either sat or stood outside the tub, rubbing the iron rods to their ailing parts. This was supposed to break up any obstructions, allowing the magnetic fluid to circulate freely.

To create just the right ambience, Mesmer frequently introduced music, specifically the sounds from something called a glass harmonica, an instrument designed by none other than Benjamin Franklin. You get a similar teeth-on-edge effect by rubbing a wet finger around the rim of a wineglass.

I'm guessing Mesmer didn't get laid a lot.

His life wasn't without its ups and downs; the downs came courtesy of the French government and the French medical profession. Both were outspokenly skeptical of Mesmer's claims and concluded, vociferously, that his cures were nothing more than the effects of his patients' rampant imaginations. He refined his technique after that, and is thought to have discovered the incredible power of suggestion.

Hard as I tried, I could find no reason anything Mesmer did two hundred years ago would promote the spate of horrifying murders of ten women today.

To be thorough, I typed in "Mesmer's Manuscripts."

This time, Google took 0.15 seconds but found only 66 entries. The most informative was from the Bakken Library and Museum. I remained diligent and checked every entry over the next few hours but found no reference to the manuscript that Eric had discovered in the attic.

I was batting zero.

Which meant the manuscript was either a fraud or it really had sat undisturbed and undiscovered in the attic for almost two hundred years.

Before I left, I took a moment and Googled STIX. One hundred and eighty-seven thousand hits in 0.11 seconds. I waded through fonts and drumsticks, pixie sticks and flower sticks, Glu-stick and Macho Stix (which turned out to be dog food) before I found Stix the paparazzi photographer. His web page was a work in progress so there wasn't much information, but there was a bunch of other people's finer moments caught on film for all the world to see. Britney Spears falling off a skateboard. Michael Jackson with his mouth open, looking white-on-white goofy. And a flurry of movie stars ducking in and out of places hoping not to be seen. At the foot of the page there was a phone number.

I made a note of it. I'd been thinking I might need some help on this one and anyone daft enough to hang off the back of a motorcycle in the rain deserves serious consideration.

I packed up my stuff, handed over the computer to a pair of spotty young nerds, who looked like porn surfers, and thanked Sandra once again for her help.

"Anytime." She fluttered her eyelids at me and her fingers brushed her lips.

I ducked out of the library before the kiss she blew my way knocked me on my ass.

Chapter Thirteen

I REACHED THE Lansdales' house. I had phoned Gina Lansdale earlier and she confirmed the translation would be ready. I could hear the clackity-clack of a typewriter as she talked on the phone. She sounded much nicer than her husband.

There were several cars parked on the street and I parked a few doors past her driveway and walked back. The rain had stopped but the wind had picked up. A motorcycle and sidecar was parked by the curb, which is the only sensible thing to do with a bike in such lousy weather.

Lansdale's house was big. Geoffrey Lansdale must charge a small fortune to represent the citizenry of St. Albans. The street was lined with dozens of mature oak trees, and most of the stately looking homes were tucked behind tall hedgerows. It was a quiet, residential neighbourhood that spoke of money and power and all the privileges associated with both. Lansdale's house was impressive with a set of wide front steps leading to a covered porch and a heavy wooden front door painted a deep, austere ruby red.

No cheap and cheery yellows here.

I rang the doorbell and Big Ben chimed deep within the house. The chimes went on for a long time but nobody answered. I stepped back and looked at the house. Nothing moved; no curtains fluttered. I stepped to one of the front windows and peered in but there was nobody there. I rang the bell again and counted a slow sixty but still no answer. I walked around the house. The garage was tucked around the back.

But halfway round, I stopped.

I could hear something, like a flag snapping in the wind. Curious, I moved down the side of the big house and around the back. A window stood open, and the curtain hung outside the frame, whipped into a wet frenzy by the wind. An old wooden box stood beneath the open window. Someone had moved it very recently. I saw a patch of dead grass where it had stood.

I moved closer.

It was an old rabbit hutch.

I thought about the rabbit's foot and wondered what bad luck waited for me on the other side of that window.

I climbed on the hutch and pushed the wet curtain aside.

And didn't like what I saw.

A broken window latch, muddy boot scuffs on the countertop and on the floor. I stepped back down and moved left, to the back door. I used the tail of my T-shirt to avoid smudging any fingerprints and tried the door handle.

It wasn't locked.

I stepped quietly inside and slipped off my shoes, squatted and studied the boot marks.

They tracked in both directions. Big feet. Really big.

Whoever came in this way had also returned.

But had they left the house?

I glanced around the kitchen. Nothing seemed to have been disturbed. Over on the counter, close to the stove, stood a knife rack. I considered taking one, an evil-looking thing with a serrated edge, but decided against it. This might be a crime scene and I had no wish to leave my fingerprints anywhere unless it was absolutely necessary. Besides, whoever might be here could construe such a weapon as justification to start something they otherwise wouldn't start. I felt comfortable with the speed of my own reflexes to keep me out of trouble.

Though I did wish it was a gun on my hip rather than a cell phone. Calling the police wasn't an option just then either. I needed that translation in my hands before I called them.

I moved soundlessly through the kitchen, staying close to the left-hand wall, past the cupboards and away from the furniture. I could see the hallway through the open door. It was in shadow. There was an oriental runner along its full length. I counted four doors, two on the left, two on the right, and a staircase at the far end, close to the front door. I could see the curve of the stairs coming down. Dark wooden spindles with a large wooden acorn topping off the heavy railing at the bottom.

I moved quietly into the hall.

Breathing silently through my mouth, I pushed the first door with my toe. It opened onto a study with a fine mahogany desk and an old-fashioned typewriter, a black Underwood. My father had owned one. Bookshelves ran from floor to ceiling and a cream-coloured, four-door filing cabinet stood against the far wall. I pushed the door all the way open.

The room was empty. Nobody lurking inside waiting to jump me.

So far, so good.

The next room on the left was a pale green-and-white two-piece bathroom. It had a fan in place of a window. There was an old pedestal washbasin, the sort that people pay a fortune for today, and a toilet with the lid up. I glanced in the mirror over the sink.

The room was empty.

Two down, two to go.

The first door across the hall was shut tight. I moved past it and touched my foot to the last door on the right. It swung inward, making a soft sigh as it brushed over the carpet. I knew it was a bedroom. It was the room I'd looked in from outside. A narrow bed, a chest of drawers, a few pictures on the wall but an air of emptiness; a spare room for the occasional guest.

I pushed the door all the way to the wall.

Empty.

Or so it seemed.

I lowered myself to the floor and lifted the bedspread. There was nothing beneath the bed.

Not even a dust bunny.

Gina Lansdale was a good housekeeper.

I backtracked to the fourth door, wrapped my T-shirt around the handle, pinched it between finger and thumb and turned it.

It opened with a click as loud as a shotgun blast.

But there was something else.

A smell.

A real stench. An overpowering mix of odors that warned of something ugly and disgusting on the other side of that door.

I stepped back and let the weight of the door swing inwards. I saw hardwood floor and the leg of a dining table.

And something else.

A foot.

A woman's foot, half out of its shoe.

I moved sideways. Gina Lansdale was lying on her right side, her dress pulled over her hips, naked from the waist down. Well, I assumed it was Gina Lansdale. She had soiled herself. The smell was overpowering in the confines of the dining room.

I moved closer, trying not to gag.

Her hands were duct-taped behind her back.

This was not the first dead body I had seen. Not by a long shot. But nothing I had seen so far could have prepared me for what he had done to her. Reading about it is one thing. Standing in the same room with it is something else entirely.

He had crushed her head to less than a quarter its normal size, and something sticky oozed along the floorboards.

It looked like blood.

Mixed with something else.

Something grey, like tapioca.

With the door pushed all the way to the wall, I could see there was no one else in the room. Gina Lansdale's head was a grotesque caricature of a human head. A watermelon of a head dropped on a sidewalk from a great height. It was a head run over by a steamroller. Even if I'd known her, I would not have recognized her from what was left of her face. It had been massively crushed, its misshapen cheeks compressed inward, one eye bulging from its socket like a hernia. Her outstretched tongue touched the floor, her lips a pouty, purple, swollen mass. A chunk of her scalp had split wide open along a fault line, front to back, and beneath it bubbled the grey brain cells, oozing out to mix with the blood on her nicely polished hardwood floor. I thought how house-proud she was and how she would feel to witness such mess.

I moved behind her and could see the whole room, through the open door into the hall.

The hallway was empty.

But there was something in the room with me, something on the floor against the wall.

It was a bag.

A long, black, heavy canvas bag.

I moved towards it even though I didn't want to. I squatted down and pried the sides apart. The interior was dark and foreboding. When I reached in, my hand recoiled. I had touched cold metal, sticky with something still warm. I pulled open the top and looked inside. Black metal pipes with screw threads on the ends. Two large, hinged plates, glistening wet, welded to a series of short metal bars.

Human skull crackers.

He was still here.

He was still in the house.

I stood up so fast, it made me light-headed. I reached for my cell. I needed police backup. I punched in the number.

Nine-one-one.

Dr. Maurice had warned me that my memory might play tricks on me after the brain beating I took last summer.

I stared at the phone pad.

Nine-one-one?

That was in North America.

But I was in England. They used different numbers here.

And while my addled brain tried desperately to recall the nine-nine-nine emergency number it needed, he was suddenly on me like a wild thing. The phone went flying as he crashed into me, sending me sideways. I was scrabbling to regain my balance. He grabbed me with both hands, curling thick leather-gloved fingers into my windpipe.

And he lifted me clean off the floor.

He was massive. Six-six and three hundred and fifty pounds. I gave away six inches and one hundred and twenty pounds.

He gave away nothing.

He wore black leather. Encased from head to toe, including a full-face crash helmet with a dark visor. The eyes that bulged hugely within the visor were mine, reflected back at me as he maintained a crushing grip on my windpipe.

I tried, God help me, to hurt him. I grabbed the helmet and attempted to twist it off his shoulders but he squeezed harder until there was no air getting into my lungs, no blood reaching my brain. I slammed my hands against his helmet, punched down towards his throat, clawed at the visor to open it, to gouge out his eyes, but he put his head down against his forearms. My blows bounced off his heavy leather jacket and I was rapidly losing strength. I crashed my foot into his groin, gained a few seconds of relief as he stepped backwards and I felt my feet touch the ground. I lashed out with my foot again and clipped his thigh but I was in stocking feet and he was in thick, durable leather.

Vivid red spots floated before my eyes. I knew I would pass out faster from a lack of blood to the brain than a lack of air to the lungs. I dug deep for one final effort and managed to jam the heel of my left hand hard under the chin of his helmet. His head slammed back, snapping open his visor and, for a crisp split second, I got a look at his face, buried deep within the helmet. His lips were flecked red with savage anger. His badly misshapen teeth were splashed with white spittle. But it was his eyes that scared me. Cold, reptilian slits where something snake-like lived, a wild thing that slithered from side to side, making my flesh crawl. A fat tongue emerged, licked wet spittle from his lips, then retreated inside that grotesque mouth. A moment later, he dropped his head forward and the visor snapped shut. He tightened his grip around my throat and rammed me backwards into the wall. It staggered me. I had never felt such overriding strength before.

I could see the next move coming but couldn't get out of the way. He pulled his head back three inches and head-butted me savagely in the face with the crash helmet.

In the last split second, I'd managed to turn my head slightly, and the blow caught me just above the left eyebrow. I went limp, feigning unconsciousness, though it didn't require much feigning. I let my body weight hang from his hands, which were around my throat. I hung there, unable to breathe, his hands blocking off my windpipe. I tried to stay focused, a losing battle. The red spots collided, expanded, then turned black as the lights went out. I barely remember the kick he delivered to my ribs after he threw me to the floor.

I lay like an embryo, fetal and warm as the blood flowed freely from the split above my eyebrow. Time softened and a great wave carried me away somewhere safe.

Regaining consciousness later was an exercise in pain management. Waves of the stuff swelled from the split above my left eye. My throat burned fiercely as if I'd swallowed a fireball. When I tried to roll onto my back, my ribs burned in agony. I hugged myself and lay still, wishing for death.

From my one good eye, I could see that the black canvas bag was no longer there.

I listened.

Had he left, too?

I thought I heard the sound of a motorcycle engine moving away. Or perhaps I imagined it, merely hoping. I drifted away again, and when I came back, the pain was sharper, more intense but also more focusing.

It took a while before I regained my feet. A pool of my own blood now stained Gina's hardwood floor.

Not that she would care anymore, God rest her soul.

I worked my way to my knees, then to my stocking feet. I held my T-shirt to the cut over my eye and scooped up my cell phone from the floor. I had to know if he had gone. I staggered to the front bedroom, looked to the street beyond the front lawn.

The motorcycle and sidecar were no longer parked by the curb.

I wondered why he hadn't killed me when he had the chance. Another ten seconds, maybe less, and I would be dead.

Perhaps he only enjoyed killing women.

If there was any good news here it was that Dr. Peter Maurice would be a free man today. And I could go home to warm chinook winds, and my E.R. nurse would bring me back to life.

I made my way down the hall to the bathroom and a sharp pain in the ball of my right foot made me wince. I gathered up a handful of toilet tissue and pressed it to my brow to help stem the flow of blood, then wobbled my way to the study with the mahogany desk and the Underwood typewriter. I looked for a copy of the manuscript. If it was worth killing Gina Lansdale for, I needed the translation before calling the police. I checked the desk drawers and the filing cabinet, not bothering to cover my prints anymore.

But there was no sign of the manuscript, or of Gina's translation, anywhere in the study.

The old Underwood stood squarely in the centre of the desk. I examined it. It had a black-over-red typing ribbon that looked fairly new. I unclipped the cover, lifted the ribbon from the spools and held it to the light. Old typewriters use the same ribbon over and over again. When the ribbon comes to an end, a lever sends the ribbon in the opposite direction. This ribbon was fairly new, so the last few words she'd typed were still partly legible, if you didn't mind reading backwards.

Through my one good eye I could read the last few words she had translated.

. . . in the year of our Lord, Eighteen Hundred and Fourteen.

So she'd finished the translation. But there was no sign of it. Technically, once Peter was released, my job was finished. But that didn't stop me wanting to know why the hell a two-hundred-year-old manuscript had gotten eleven people killed.

Eleven and a half, including me.

I opened the cell phone and punched in nine-nine-nine.

"What is the nature of your emergency?" a woman asked.

I tried to speak, but he'd squashed my windpipe, and the word "police" sounded horrible, like "porridge." I tried again. On the third attempt, I managed to make her understand. I coughed up the address, literally, and had to sit down to wait for my head to stop spinning.

"Do you wish to stay on the line until the police arrive?" she asked.

I shook my head and hung up.

Dumb move.

My head spun one way while the room spun the other.

Chapter Fourteen

BEFORE THE POLICE ARRIVED, I took stock. The split above my left eye would take a dozen stitches. My throat was sore, and swallowing was excruciating, but that would pass. My ribs hurt like a son of a bitch. I tested them by stretching until I felt reasonably sure they weren't broken. All in all, I'd gotten away lightly. I had never felt such unbelievable strength in my life.

And it scared the hell out of me.

As my head cleared, I began to wonder about things. How did he know Gina Lansdale had the manuscript? If it was so important that he felt compelled to kill for it, I needed to reach Sylvia Maurice. The second copy was under my mattress in the spare bedroom.

Such madness.

How could he know I had a copy?

Before the police arrived, I phoned Sylvia. The answering machine kicked in. Sylvia's voice apologized that neither she nor Peter could come to the phone, then encouraged me to leave a message. I told her to call me immediately and gave her my cell phone number.

"It's very, very urgent," I added and hung up.

The police arrived a minute later. A pair of uniformed officers, both in their twenties. They viewed me suspiciously. I tried to stem the bleeding with a fresh wad of tissue.

"You might not want to go in there," I said, pointing at the closed door of Gina Lansdale's dining room.

I stood back while they ignored my advice and stared in horror at Gina's remains.

"Christ!" one of them said, his hand clamped quickly to his mouth.

He had the good sense to run outside where he threw up in the bushes. His partner looked as though he might do the same.

"I tried to warn you," I said, not unkindly, and he nodded.

"We had to see for ourselves," he said. "You found her like this?"

"Yes."

"You haven't touched anything, have you?"

"Nothing." I shook my head, then regretted it. "He was still in the house when I got here," I said. "He attacked me."

The policeman stared at me, then called his partner.

"Joel!"

His partner came back looking bad.

"He might still be in the house," the policeman said. He nodded at me. "He saw him."

They unsnapped their nightsticks. I think they call them

truncheons. They were tense, looking up and down the hallway. Why the hell the Brits don't arm their policemen, I'll never know. A couple of Sidewinder ground-to-air missiles would take the bastard out.

"I'm pretty sure he's gone," I said.

The one named Joel asked me what was wrong with my voice.

"Tried to strangle me. He was all in leather. I think he rides a motorbike with a sidecar. He head-butted me in the face with his helmet." They looked at me with a mixture of awe and pity. "He was large," I said, trying to regain a little dignity. "Six-six, three hundred and fifty pounds."

They stared at me.

"Did you get a look at him?" Joel asked.

"No. He had a dark visor. I couldn't see his face."

I had already decided against telling them what I saw. It was a blinding, split-second flash of a face distorted by the helmet.

But a face that would stay with me forever.

They put me in the spare room where I sat on the bed and tried not to bleed on the bedspread. They searched the house looking for the man the press called the Crusher. When they came back empty-handed, I told them I was going to drive myself to the hospital but they insisted, officially, that I stay put.

An unmarked police car arrived next. It turned into the yard with a squeal of tires, and four plainclothes officers piled out. It wasn't much of a stretch to figure out which one was Detective Inspector Gerry Newcombe. He led the other three into the house. He glanced into the guest bedroom but, even though he saw me, he never slowed his pace. I could hear him talking with the young officers down the hall. I heard a couple of "Jesus H. Christs" before he came to see me.

He pushed the door closed.

He was a tall, thin man with hollow cheeks and narrow eyes that took in the whole room before stopping on me. Hard to know his age, but I'd guess he was already on the wrong side of fifty. He had the kind of five o'clock shadow you just knew had always been a problem. He wore a dark blue trench coat and carried a hat. His tie looked greasy and the collar of his shirt curled up at the points. The first and second fingers of his right hand were heavily stained a dirty yellow. This man didn't believe in filter-tipped cigarettes. And he chewed his fingernails. He stared at me while I bled into a fresh wad of tissue.

"What happened here?" He stood right over me, far too close for comfort.

"Sit down," I said. "Over there." I pointed to the vacant chair, but he ignored me, so I ignored him right back.

"I won't ask you again." He spoke through gritted teeth, looking straight at me.

"It hurts to lift my head," I told him. "And I'm damned if I'm going to talk to your crotch. So, either back up to where I can see you, or go and sit your ass down."

He took a moment, then backed up a couple of feet.

"I had an appointment with Gina Lansdale at four o'clock today," I said.

"Geoffrey Lansdale's wife?"

"Yes."

"You're sure that's her?"

"No. I've never met her. But it's a pretty safe bet that's who she is. Or was."

"What were you seeing her about?"

"She's my client's lawyer's wife," I said.

"I know who she is," he snapped. "Why were you coming to see her?"

"None of your damn business," I snapped. "When she didn't answer the front door, I went around the back. Somebody'd moved a rabbit hutch under the kitchen window. The window had been forced open, muddy footprints over the kitchen counter, all over the floor. I went in through the back door. It was unlocked. I found Gina's body. I also found a black canvas bag in the room with her. About four feet long, eighteen inches square. I opened it. It was full of metal pipes, a hinged set of semicircular plates. It was sticky with blood. So I knew he was still in the house."

"Why didn't you call the police?"

"I tried. He came up behind me. Took me by surprise."

I didn't like the sneer on Detective Inspector Newcombe's face but I let it go for now.

"And?"

"He tried to strangle me. I tried to fight him off but he had both hands around my throat. Then he butted me in the face. He was wearing a crash helmet. I passed out. He dropped me, kicked me in the ribs, then left. End of story."

"I'll decided when the story's ended," he said. "What did he look like?"

"Six-six, three hundred and fifty pounds, not much of it fat. Head to toe in leather. Good quality stuff, thick, all black, even his boots. Full-face Shoei crash helmet with a dark visor. I thought dark visors were illegal over here."

He didn't answer.

"Leather gloves." I continued. "And he's incredibly strong."

He raised an eyebrow.

"He lifted me off the floor."

Newcombe looked me over, assessing the strength of a man who could lift one hundred and eighty-five pounds off the floor by the neck.

"Would you recognize him again?"

"No."

"That's bloody convenient," he said and, at the time, I didn't understand what he meant.

"I'm pretty sure he rides a black motorbike with a side-car."

We were interrupted by one of the other plainclothes officers.

"Geoffrey Lansdale's here, sir."

Newcombe gave me a hard, flat look.

"Don't you move," he said and left me sitting on the bed.

I heard him talking with Geoffrey on the front porch. I stood up carefully, then made my way to the kitchen, retrieved my shoes and carried them through the house. The two men were still on the front porch.

Newcombe had obviously given Geoffrey the bad news. He looked ghastly and he was leaning against the side of the porch as I put my shoes on and pushed past the two uniformed policemen.

"Geoffrey," I said. "I'm so very sorry."

Geoffrey Lansdale looked at me without seeing me. His eyes were glazed over. He was taking the news very hard. "If there's anything I can do, please let me know."

"I told you to wait." Newcombe glowered at me.

"I need to get to the hospital." I moved the sodden mesh of blood-soaked tissue, and Lansdale refocused suddenly. "Or are you going to continue to refuse me medical attention?"

Lansdale looked suddenly appalled at my condition.

"My God, Dancer!" he said. "What happened to you?"

"I came too late," I told him. "He was still in your house. He jumped me."

"You have to take this man to the hospital," Geoffrey said to Newcombe.

"We will," Newcombe said, not very convincingly.

"Now!" Geoffrey bellowed, and I caught a glimpse of a tough courtroom brawler.

Score one for Geoffrey. Maybe he wasn't such a bad old fart after all.

Newcombe looked angrily first in my direction, then at the policemen who'd taken my statement. "Take him. Both of you. Don't let him out of your sight. Take him down to the nick the moment they are done with him."

I pushed past him, since he hadn't moved to let me through. Joel took my elbow, but I snatched my arm away.

"You just drive, Sunshine," I said.

When they got me in the back of their car, I told Joel to lower the window in case it was my turn to throw up.

I wasn't kidding.

Chapter Fifteen

DR. RUPERT RANBAR, the attending physician in Emergency Admitting, looked barely old enough to be there without his mother. He peered curiously at my swollen brow and inquired how I came by it.

"Crash helmet," I told him.

He looked like he didn't believe me.

"From the outside in."

"Say again, please?"

"I got hit in the head by a crash helmet."

"Ah." He nodded as if the world now made sense to him.

"Do you have any allergies?" This from an elderly nurse who arrived to take my blood pressure.

Including the uniformed policemen, it was getting a bit crowded in the room.

"Needles," I said.

I considered adding crushed skulls, bone chips, brain matter and leather-clad giants with bad teeth, but decided against it.

Dr. Ranbar asked me to take off my shirt and ran his

cold fingers over my damaged rib cage. He listened to my breathing for a while before declaring that I probably hadn't broken any ribs but they should maybe take an X-ray to be sure. Could I come back tomorrow?

Then he asked the attending policemen to wait outside while he put a dozen stitches across my brow. Towards the end, I began to feel really woozy and rather sick and I finally couldn't keep from throwing up. Not once but repeatedly, which gave the doctor cause for concern.

Me, too.

"I think you might have a concussion," he said. "We'll need to keep you in overnight. For observation."

Overnight?

I didn't think so.

"Can you give Tweedledee and Tweedledum the good news?" I pointed towards the hallway.

He nodded, scribbled something on my chart and handed it to the nurse.

"I'll check on you later." He patted my shoulder. "And I thought crash helmets were supposed to protect you." He chuckled before leaving.

Ah.

East Indian humour.

My nurse's nametag read Maureen and she sat me in a wheelchair and wheeled me off to a private room down the corridor. She gave me fresh pajamas and a bathrobe and lowered the bed, making sure I was comfortably tucked in, all under the ever-watchful eyes of Tweedledee and Tweedledum, whom she insisted were to remain in the hallway.

"Here," she said, handing me a pair of Dixie cups, one

with two white pills in the bottom, the other with a few drops of water. "If you can keep these down, they'll help with the pain."

I choked them down with the three drops of water in the Dixie cup.

"Don't stand up too quickly," she said. "Percocet can make your head spin." She turned to go, then stopped and asked, "You don't have a mobile phone with you, do you?"

"Yes."

"Best turn it off," she said. "Can't use your mobile within a hundred feet of the hospital."

I turned off my cell phone.

"Is there a phone I can use?"

She told me there was one down the hall and helped me out of bed. She offered me the wheelchair and I accepted. No point in letting the Tweedles know that I was perfectly capable of walking in a straight line. We set off at a leisurely pace, the two cops shuffling along behind us.

"So what have you done?" Maureen asked, glancing over her shoulder.

I shook my head.

Ouch.

You think I'd never learn.

"I haven't done anything. It's those two. I'm keeping them under surveillance for impersonating police officers."

Nobody was using the phone. I waved the cops back a full twenty feet before I called Sylvia's house. The line was busy. I hung up, counted to thirty, tried again.

She caught it on the second ring.

"Hello?"

"Sylvia?"

"Oh, Edward!" She sounded upset. "I was trying to call you. What are we going to do?"

"About what?" I asked.

"About Peter."

Peter?

"Have you heard what happened to Gina Lansdale?" I said.

"Yes. They told me. It's just awful."

"I was there." I lowered my voice to a whisper. "In the house with him."

"You saw him?" She sounded incredulous.

"Yes. He jumped me. Choked me. Split my head open. I'm in the hospital. They've just stitched me up. Can you come and get me?"

"Oh, Edward. I'm so, so sorry."

"Can you come?"

"Yes. Of course."

"Can you bring the binder?"

"What binder?"

"The manuscript. It's in my room. Under the mattress," I said, and felt stupid telling her that.

"I'll come right away."

"I think the binder's very important," I stressed. "You will bring it with you?"

"Yes, of course I will."

"Are the paparazzi still there?"

"Yes. Always."

"Okay. Do what you can. I'll make sure someone meets you when you get here. Come to Emergency Admitting."

"Oh, dear, Edward. I'm so sorry we have caused you all this trouble."

"Well, if there is a bright side," I said, "at least it proves that Peter is innocent. We can get him out now."

"Oh." There was a pause. "Then you haven't heard?"

"Heard what?"

A longer pause.

"I'll tell you when I see you, Edward," and before I could ask her what she meant, she'd hung up.

And that drove me crazy, wondering what the hell was going on.

Chapter Sixteen

SYLVIA ARRIVED FORTY minutes later. By then, the painkiller had kicked in and I felt like Alice in Wonderland. Tweedledee and Tweedledum prevented the press from following Sylvia to my room, and she sat on a brown fake leather armchair across from my bed. She put the binder on the nightstand next to me

"You look awful," she said, which didn't go a long way to making me feel much better. "I'm so very sorry, Edward. It must really hurt."

"They gave me something for it," I said, feeling pretty fantastic and ready to go home with her. "So tell me, what have I missed?"

She sat forward in the chair, leaning in with her news.

"This morning, when Geoffrey came, he called a special meeting with a local judge. He posted bail and they released Peter shortly after one o'clock this afternoon."

"That's great," I said, astonished that he'd posted bail. "So where is he now?"

She looked at me, a look full of hurt. "He didn't come

back to the house," she said. "He couldn't face the paparazzi." Her chin went all loose and wobbly. "He slipped away from them at the police station and went for a long walk. He called me, said he needed to be by himself for a while. I think being locked up really scared him."

"Where is he now?"

She looked up, her eyes red and puffy.

"He's been arrested again. He called me. He's back in jail."

Now I understood Newcombe's remark about how convenient it was that I hadn't seen my attacker's face.

"They think Peter killed Gina Lansdale?"

She was biting her lip and nodding.

I thought about that for a moment. Peter knew Geoffrey's wife was translating the manuscript because I'd told him, in code, that morning. He also knew I was picking it up at four o'clock. He had opportunity because he was free on bail. And he was unaccounted for. But it clearly wasn't Peter Maurice who'd head-butted me. It was a man one hundred and seventy pounds heavier and eight inches taller. Besides, I saw enough of his face to know it wasn't Peter Maurice. But that raised another question. How did the man who attacked me know Peter was out on bail? Had he set it up to throw suspicion on Peter? Or was it coincidental? Or was Peter in cahoots with the man they called the Crusher?

Impossible.

Yet how did the Crusher know Gina Lansdale had a copy of the manuscript?

The only answer that made sense was that Peter was

somehow involved. Was it voluntary or involuntary?

Was he being blackmailed?

Or was he the blackmailer?

Or was I missing something?

"How did he make bail?" I asked.

She bit her lip and shook her head.

"I don't know," she said and looked away.

There was something she wasn't telling me. Before I could broach the subject, there was a knock at the door and Joel, the policeman with the sensitive stomach, stuck his head inside.

"We're off," he said.

"Off?"

"Yeah. Apparently you don't warrant an escort anymore."

"You're not being replaced?"

"No. Good night, ma'am." He nodded at Sylvia.

He let the door swing slowly shut.

"Were they guarding you?" Sylvia asked.

"No. They were just making sure I didn't escape." I decided to quit while I was ahead. "Where's your car?"

"Outside in the parking lot," she said. "When I saw that you hadn't taken it, I drove myself home."

"Where's the paparazzi?"

"Everywhere," she said with a sigh. "Most of them followed me here."

"Let's find a back way out. We'll take a cab if we have to."

"I thought they were keeping you in overnight?"

"I'm discharging myself."

She looked away while I took off the pajamas and found

my clothes. My T-shirt was caked in blood. I grabbed the binder from the nightstand.

"Ready?"

She took my arm and we sidled down the hallway, taking the stairs to the basement to avoid the front desk. We followed a maze of corridors to the rear of the building, then up a metal staircase to a loading area. From there, we saw an EXIT sign that took us straight out the back of the hospital. A chill wind was blowing and we followed a winding footpath through a rose garden and up onto a busy street. We crossed the street and walked up the hill. The hospital parking lot was on our left.

Sylvia's Ford was parked near the end of the row. There were no paparazzi lurking nearby that we could see.

But they didn't need to lurk.

Someone had parked a car right behind Sylvia's, blocking her in so they could all go wait in the warm.

"Bastards," I said. "Give me the keys."

We walked quickly across the road, down a few steps to the far end of the parking lot. I unlocked the big Ford, let Sylvia in on the passenger side out of the wind, then went and checked out the car behind us. It was smaller than the Ford. A two-door. I peered through the driver's side window. It had a stick shift. I hoped it was in neutral and only on its parking brake.

I hurried to the Ford, climbed in, fired up the motor and dropped it in reverse.

"Hold tight," I told her and eased off the brake.

We rolled back a foot before we touched the other car's bumper. I gassed it and felt the car behind me start to give.

The Ford began to spin its tires. I moved forward, dropped it into reverse and backed into the little two-door at no more than five miles an hour.

Then all hell broke loose.

Five miles an hour was all it took to trigger the other car's alarm.

And inflate its air bags.

The scream of the dual-tone alarm cut the air like a banshee, drawing everyone's attention. I stood on the gas pedal, burned off the water beneath the tires until they bit into hot, dry asphalt and physically shunted the car behind me backwards twenty-five feet. I came off the gas, dropped the Ford in drive and peeled away from the car behind us.

We drove past the emergency entrance as the paparazzi came pouring out. They broke into a run but by then we were on the main road. I turned fast into heavy traffic. A sharp right across the front of an oncoming bus and we were down a side street. A bunch more lefts and rights and we were all alone. I slowed at the end of a short hill, recognized my surroundings and drove us sedately home. I parked in the parking lot south of the house and locked the binder in the trunk of the car.

I still couldn't call it the boot.

There were only a few paparazzi on watch as we approached the gate. We battled the usual burst of flashbulbs and pleas for sound bites and hurried up the walk to the front door. There were no policemen in attendance, which meant the paparazzi would probably become bolder.

Once inside, Sylvia made tea while I made sure the house was secure. I checked all the windows and doors and closed the drapes so there were no cracks. Within minutes, the front doorbell chimed. We ignored it. After a few more rings and a few heavy knocks on the door, they gave up for the night.

The painkiller was making my head spin. I sat down and watched the ten o'clock news. Peter made the headlines again.

"This is just awful," Sylvia said. She turned off the television and we sat quietly for several long minutes before she spoke again. "You should get some sleep," she said.

She was right. The jet lag, the adrenal rush, the blood loss, the drugs, dealing with the death of Gina Lansdale, it all conspired to exhaust me. I wanted to ask her about Peter, about why they released him the first time, but I didn't trust myself not to make a mess of it. I decided it could wait until morning.

I said good night and made my way up to my room. The stitches looked angry and I wondered if my eye would close up by morning. I brushed my teeth, plumped the pillow and climbed into bed.

A weary defective detective.

Day two and still batting zero.

I laid my head down and tried to let my mind go blank. At first, it wasn't easy, but then the drug began to take over and I felt euphoric. My eyes closed and I began to doze off.

It was maybe ten minutes before I heard the sound.

I lay still, feigning sleep.

Someone pushed my bedroom door open and light from the hall seeped into my room. I cracked open my one good eye half a millimetre.

She was wearing a short, silk nightie under an open housecoat. Her long thigh muscles looked taut as bowstrings.

"Edward?" So quiet, I scarcely heard her.

She moved forward, the silk top rustling in the dark. I lay still, my left arm resting outside the comforter. She came to the edge of the bed. I could smell her perfume.

"Hi."

"You're awake?" she said, her voice soft and fragile.

"Yes."

"Can I stay with you tonight?"

She reached down and tugged the covers back but I kept my arm by my side, holding them in place.

"I can't be alone, Edward," she said. "Not tonight."

She sat on the bed, facing me, her breasts so close, her dark nipples flirting with silk. My breathing was shallow, my throat constricted.

"Sylvia." I spoke quietly. "How did Peter make bail?"

That's me, all business.

She looked at me, took a shuddery breath, sobbed once and then let the real tears fall. Hard to hold back real tears. I reached out to my right and found a box of tissues.

"Oh, God." She wiped away tears, blew her nose. "Can we not talk about this right now? Can't you just hold me?"

I sat up and put what I hoped was a brotherly arm around her sisterly shoulder. She sank forward and sobbed hard and I could feel her eyelashes brushing against my neck. I held her like that for several minutes, until she got herself under control.

She sat up straight.

"He admitted seeing one of the women," she said at last. "Paula Webb." The name was familiar. She had worked in one of the bookstores where Peter was holding a signing. The third one to die. "She flirted with him," she said. "They went back to her place afterwards. He had dinner with her. Then he . . ." She paused. "He had sex with her." She gave the word "sex" a hard, bitter edge. "They found his fingerprints. He confessed to seeing her. He said he left her around ten o'clock that night. And she was still very much alive. A neighbour saw him leave. The neighbour spoke to Paula shortly after."

"I'm sorry." I handed her more tissue. "That doesn't seem very fair to you."

"No." She lifted her head. "Not very fair at all. And it makes me wonder about the other women."

"Which other women?"

"You think this was the first?"

"Maybe."

"Then you're a bigger fool than I am." She straightened her top, smoothed it over her breasts. I tried not to watch. "He said it didn't mean anything. Said it was just casual sex."

"Maybe that's all it was," I said, wondering why I was defending him.

"In that case —" She began to remove her housecoat until I caught hold of her wrist.

"Two wrongs don't make a right."

"You think this is wrong?"

"Yes. For both of us."

"You're not married."

"It's still wrong," I said.

She sat there looking forlorn, rejected twice in the same day. I needed to soften the damage.

"Sylvia." I took her hand. "You are a very beautiful woman." I looked her in the eye. "Making love to you would be incredible. And incredibly easy. But afterwards, we would both feel really bad. You, because a revenge fuck just isn't part of your nature, and me, because I'm seeing someone I really care about. And you are still married to Peter."

"It's his own fault," she said. "He deserves it."

"But I don't."

She blinked at me.

"Oh," she said.

She thought about that for a moment, her hands resting in her lap, her back straight, head tilted slightly. Then she became contrite and folded her arms across her breasts.

"And I can't quit the case right now," I said. "There's a man out there who can't stop killing people. And that man is not Peter."

"I'm sorry." She blew her nose again. "I feel very stupid," she said. "And very embarrassed."

"Don't be."

"I've been such an idiot."

"No. You haven't."

She sat for a while without saying anything, then finally bent forward and kissed me lightly on the forehead. Her lips felt cool against my skin. It would have been so easy to lift the covers at that moment, to let her slip inside.

"Good night, Edward."

"Good night, Sylvia."

"Friends?" She lifted my chin.

"The best of."

I curled my hand into a fist and popped her playfully on the shoulder. I watched her leave, watched her pull the door closed behind her, watched the darkness envelop me. I tried to put her out of my mind, tried to get to sleep but it was next to impossible.

Morning couldn't come soon enough.

Chapter Seventeen

FRIDAY MORNING.

I woke up needing a gun.

And an aspirin.

The gun had to have enough power to put a bullet through a crash helmet, the aspirin enough power to blow a hole in the headache behind my left eye. I'd risen early and was out of the house by six-thirty, well before Sylvia woke up. I found aspirin in the bathroom medicine cabinet.

But no gun.

Sylvia had left the ski mask I'd given Geoffrey Lansdale on a chair beside the front door. I decided against wearing it. My eyebrow hurt like hell and the thought of something rubbing against it made me cringe. I dressed to go jogging and I set my baseball hat at a jaunty angle, hoping to hide much of my face. The moment I set foot outside the door, the paparazzi rushed me. I was suddenly the new media darling.

"Come on, Eddie!" someone yelled. "Gizza quote!"

"Over here, Eddie!"

"This way, Mr. Dancer!"

They crowded the gate, cameras on zoom. They even had a couple of TV remote camera vans parked out front.

"What happened to your 'ead?" someone yelled.

"Did his old lady do that?" someone heckled.

They laughed at that. I looked over at the heckler.

"No. Yours did. She closed her legs too fast."

An old joke, and it got a bigger laugh than it really deserved.

"Not my old lady," the heckler said. "She'd never open 'em that wide!"

Ah, the merry banter.

But it gave me a chance to check them out. Stix was still there, firing off roll after roll in my direction. I pulled my baseball hat low over my eyes and set off at a brisk trot up the road towards the cathedral. I heard engines firing up behind me. At the entrance to the lake, I picked up speed and jogged across the open grass. A few of the hardier ones gave chase but they were hampered by their equipment and weren't dressed for jogging on wet grass. Within a quarter mile, I had left them far behind. Thank God for that. The ball of my foot ached. I should have asked the doctor to take a look at it last night but he'd have poked me with a needle and I'd had my fill of them. I slowed to a fast walk. A man and a woman were watching the ducks on the lake but they were too far away to overhear me. I took out my cell phone, punched in the country code for Canada and dialed a number I knew by heart.

I heard a phone ring eight thousand miles away.

"What?"

It was Nosher.

Or Splosher.

They were twins, born and bred in the east end of London but living now on an acreage southwest of Calgary with a beautiful view of the Rocky Mountains. I had a momentary pang of homesickness.

"I need a gun," I said.

"You've got a bleedin' gun," he replied.

"I need one in England."

"England?"

"Yes. Your old manor."

"Is that where you are?"

"Yes. A place called St. Albans."

"Write down this number," he said, all business.

I wrote it down.

"Who do I ask for?"

"Nobody. When it stops ringing, leave your phone number. Someone will call you back."

"That's it?"

"What do you want? A bleedin' catalogue?" he said and hung up.

I called the number he gave me. It rang once and stopped, though nobody answered. I recited my cell number, hung up and waited. It rang in less than a minute.

"Hello?" I answered.

"What do you need?" A man's voice, thin and reedy, distorted by an electronic gadget.

"A gun," I said.

"Of course you do," he said, humouring me. "What sort?"

"Nine millimetre. SIG. Glock. Beretta."

"Your choice," he said.

"The SIG, then. I need it today."

"Three hundred quid," he said.

"With an extra clip, fully loaded."

"Three-fifty."

I didn't argue.

"When and where?"

"Keep yer phone on," he said and hung up.

I looked around the lake wondering if anyone had overheard me place an order for an illegal firearm. I put the phone away and limped southwards. I found a taxi and directed him down London Road, a long hill plastered with shops and offices on both sides. We drove past the Hertz office where my block of cheese waited patiently out front. I had the cabbie drop me at Geoffrey Lansdale's house. There was a police cruiser parked across the driveway, the house roped off with yellow crime scene tape. The uniforms in the cruiser, cold and bored, watched me as I unlocked the rented Mercedes and climbed in. The aspirin wasn't doing much for my headache. I fired up the motor and pulled away slowly. They watched me leave. There was no sign of a motorcycle, with or without a sidecar. As I drove away, I passed a car driven by a woman with a male companion.

And I knew exactly who they were.

I picked up a morning paper from a box near the library and read it over coffee in a nearby café. It was full of pictures of Peter, with banner headlines about Gina's murder and Peter's second arrest. I drank more coffee and waited until the library opened at nine o'clock.

Sandra spotted me coming through the doors and I wondered if she'd been lurking close by, waiting for my return.

"Well, hello again," she said, beaming. "How can I help you this morning?" Then she saw the stitches. "Oh, my! What happened to you?"

"A crash helmet fell on me," I answered, honestly.

"It looks very sore."

I shrugged it off, the strong, silent type, and explained what I wanted this time. She walked me to a computer terminal and proceeded to type faster than the speed of light, her chubby fingers flying over the keys.

"Italian, you said?" She rested her fingers on my sleeve.

"Old Italian," I stressed.

"That's right," she said.

She stayed busy. I watched the screen over her shoulder. Names, addresses, phone numbers.

"There's quite a lot," I said.

"Yes, there are."

"Can you trim them down a bit?"

"How?"

"Just southern England?" I asked.

"That's easy enough."

She hit a few keys and the list shrank to something more manageable. She hit the print key and handed me a list, two and a half pages long, of the names and addresses of translators specializing in Old Italian.

"There you go." She stood up and squeezed her face into a smile.

"Thank you, Sandra," I said. "You're an angel."

She expected more, so I took the unbaked loaf that was her right hand and kissed it, backing away before she swooned and fell on top of me.

"You take good care, now," she called as I pushed through the main doors onto the street.

I drove to the parking lot near Sylvia's house, coming in from the south so the paparazzi wouldn't see me. It had stopped raining and the sun peeked through the clouds, putting a smile on everyone's face.

Okay, a grimace.

I'd already decided I needed help on this one. I didn't know the country well enough to navigate with any real sense of confidence and I needed a good backup, a good resource person on my side. I could have called Danny Many-Guns in Calgary but I felt I needed someone who knew the lay of the land.

Time for Plan A.

I flipped the cell phone open and punched in Stix's phone number from his web page.

It barely rang.

"Hi, this is Stix. Leave a message."

I hung up. I didn't want to leave my cell number because he might call me at an inconvenient time. Besides, if he turned me down, he still had my cell number.

On to Plan B.

At the back of the parking lot, a young man was tinkering under the hood of the orange-and-green shagging wagon. He emerged long enough to give me a quick once-over before ducking back under the hood. He looked to be about eighteen.

I found a pen in my glovebox and printed a note on a piece of paper, folded in into quarters and wrapped it in a twenty-pound note. I climbed from the car and walked to the van.

"What's the problem?" I said.

He stayed bent and looked over his shoulder. His long hair fell over the side of his face. It was died a horrible orange to match the van.

"I'm not fixing it," he said, very belligerent. "I'm checking the oil."

"I don't care."

He looked at me a long moment.

"You're not the parking dude?"

"Nope."

He straightened up, a wrench in his hand. His face was red with acne that clashed with the colour of his hair. There was a smear of grease across his forehead. He tossed his hair out of his face.

"You sure?"

"I'm sure I'm sure."

"They gave me grief last week," he said. "Just for changing the plugs."

"I'm not here to give you grief. I'm here to give you money."

I held out the twenty to him.

"What's that for?" he asked, suspicious.

"I need you to walk up there." I pointed up the street. "There's a bunch of paparazzi outside one of the houses."

"Yeah? The woman what lives there? Her old man killed all them women."

I wasn't going to argue.

"There's a guy there, rides the back of a motorcycle. A big BMW. His name's Stix. Think you could find him, slip him this note without anyone noticing?"

"What's it say?"

I opened it up.

CHRISTOPHER'S. 15 MIN. E.D.

"What's it mean?

"It means you make twenty quid for five minutes work. Less if you walk fast."

"I'm not gonna get arrested, am I?"

"Not unless they've passed a law against really bad hair," I said.

"I dunno." He hesitated.

I folded the money around the note.

"You keep working on your car," I said. "I'll find somebody else."

"I never said I wouldn't," he said, moody.

"You never said you would."

He wiped his hands on the back of his jeans and took the money with the note.

"What's he look like, this fellah?"

It was hard to tell. I'd only seen him in a crash helmet or in a hoodie.

"Ask his driver," I said. "He stays with the bike. He'll point him out to you. But be surreptitious."

"Be what?"

"Inconspicuous."

"Right." He nodded, but still looked mystified.

"I don't want anyone to see you slipping him the note,"

I said. "Okay?"

"Yeah. Inconspicuous. I got it the first time."

"Give me the keys."

"To what?"

"The van."

"Fuck off, why would I do that?"

"How'd I know you'll deliver the note without some incentive?"

"How'd I know you won't drive off in my van?"

"You've got to be joking," I said. "I wouldn't be seen dead driving it."

"You still ain't getting the keys."

"All right. But if you don't deliver the note, I'll flatten your tires."

"It's a lot of bleedin' trouble for twenty miserable quid."

"Oh, it's no trouble," I assured him.

I watched him slouch away up the hill. Once he was out of sight, I went to Sylvia's Ford, unlocked the trunk and retrieved the binder. I walked across the street and cut towards the town centre on a parallel road, away from the paparazzi. I kept looking over my shoulder. I was looking for a motorbike and sidecar.

I felt naked and very vulnerable without a gun.

Chapter Eighteen

HE CAME ALONE. He saw me at the table in Christopher's Inn, sitting along the wall, and came over like it was no big thing. He unzipped his raincoat, threw back the hood and sat down across the table from me. He was about my age, mid-thirties, but where my skin was baby smooth, his was lined and well lived-in. His hair was long and straggly beneath a black headband that was hung with an assortment of metal: a crucifix, a tiny six-pointed star, a circle within a circle and rows of coloured metal beads were all interwoven into his headband. It was a good look for him.

He was skinny too.

Just like Keith Richards.

"Coffee?" the waitress asked and we nodded.

She poured us both a cup from a stainless steel carafe, left a folded bill between us on the table and moved away.

"So?" He drank it black, no sugar.

"You know who I am?"

"Sure."

"Your name is Stix?"

He smiled, a secret grin really, figuring he was on to something bigger than what he'd been waiting for, standing around with the others.

"Actually, it's Donovan Stickley but I've been Stix since I was this big." He held his finger and thumb an inch apart.

"I may need some help," I told him. "Are you as good as you look?"

"I'm better."

"And you'll work free of charge?"

"Depends."

"It'll be an exclusive," I told him.

"It'll need to be that," he said.

We were looking across the table, weighing up one another, when my cell phone rang. He recognized the signature tune and gave me a quick grin. I flipped the phone open.

"Hello?"

"Elephant & Castle. Twelve o'clock."

"Hang on."

"You wannit or not?" The man on the phone was getting antsy.

"Yes. I just don't know where that is." I left the mouthpiece uncovered. "Can we make the Elephant and Castle by noon?"

He never even checked the time.

"Not a chance. Two o'clock, maybe."

"How's two o'clock?" I asked the man on the phone.

"No," he said. "Six o'clock, then."

"All right."

Click.

I put the cell phone away. Stix was holding his coffee high so that his eyes were level across the brim of the cup.

"You know you're being followed?" he asked. "Couple of plodders." He indicated with his head. "Over there. Trying to look like newlyweds."

I knew they were there. They'd been following me all morning. They were pretending to watch the ducks on the lake when I ordered the SIG. Then getting caught when I drove by them outside Lansdale's house. There were two more following them as backup.

I was impressed that Stix had made them.

He sat back and considered me from across the table.

"What do you need me for?" he asked.

"Colour. Background. General information. Direction."

"You're here on your own?"

"Yes."

"Who gave you that?" He bobbed his head towards the evil stitching over my eye.

"He did."

"Who did?"

"You call him the Crusher."

"We call him Dr. Peter Maurice."

"It wasn't Dr. Peter Maurice who murdered Gina Lansdale."

"You saw him?"

"I saw him, felt him, smelt him and tasted him. It wasn't Peter."

"When did you meet him?"

"I was in Gina Lansdale's house right after he killed her. He carries his appliance, his skull crusher, in a black canvas bag. I saw it. He stands six feet six, weighs well over three hundred pounds, wears leather and rides a motorcycle with a sidecar. He wears a full-face Shoei helmet. He was wearing it when he delivered a full-face head-butt that just missed caving in my skull."

"It's called a Glaswegian handshake," he said. "Did he kill her like the others?"

"I never saw the others."

"But he crushed her skull?"

I nodded.

"And he attacked you?"

"Yes."

"What were you doing there?"

"Are you in?"

"This is just between you and me? No other journos?"

"Just you and me," I said.

"No holding back?"

"No holding back."

"Okay." He nodded and the metal bangles in his hair jangled like wind chimes. "I'm in."

"Good."

He drained his coffee, signalled the waitress for a refill. He propped his elbows on the table.

"So," he said. "What's it all about, Alfie?"

Chapter Nineteen

I DECIDED TO TELL HIM virtually everything. Pretty much, anyway. He didn't need to know about Sylvia's midnight confession but he did need to know about Maria and Eric's trip to Germany, about how they found the manuscript and smuggled it back to England. And I told him that the police believed it was the manuscript that got Maria killed.

"You don't happen to read Old Italian, do you?" I asked him.

He shook his head. "Why?"

He'd had no idea the manuscript even existed. The police had been very thorough in keeping it to themselves. I showed him my copy of the letter from Maria, told him about my trip to see Eric Glossard and about the two copies of the manuscript.

"Geoffrey Lansdale is Peter Maurice's lawyer. Geoffrey's wife was born in Italy. She was translating the manuscript for me."

"Did you get it translated?"

"No," I said. "He took everything with him."

"You had two copies, though?"

I picked the binder up off the chair next to me, placed it in front of him. You'd think it was the Dead Sea Scrolls. He turned the pages almost reverently.

"You don't know what any of this says?"

"No. But I intend to find out," I said. I pulled the list of translators from my pocket. "Which one of these is the closest?"

He scanned the names and addresses.

"This one," he said, flipping to the first page. "Barnet. We can stop there on the way to the Elephant and Castle."

He had picked a woman translator.

"Pick someone else," I said. "Pick a man."

He ran his finger down the list and found a man named Derick B. Thomas who lived in a place called Hendon.

"It's on the way," Stix assured me.

I dialed Derick B. Thomas's number and he answered on the fourth ring. I introduced myself and asked if he had time to translate thirty pages of Italian for me. He paused a moment before answering.

"Italian?" he asked.

"Yes. Old Italian. Early eighteen hundreds."

"For when?" he asked.

"Soon as you can."

"Can you bring it to me?"

"Yes."

"When?"

"Today. In a couple of hours." I raised a questioning eyebrow at Stix, who nodded.

"I can take a look," he said, not promising more than that.

I double-checked his address and told him I would see him later. Stix continued to turn the pages of the binder.

"You really think this is why all those people have been killed?"

"I don't know." I shrugged. "The police seem to think so. And so does the man who killed them."

"You're the detective," he said. "What do you think?"

"I think it may be worth more than the three grand Peter Maurice paid for it. I think somebody wants the original and they are prepared to frame Peter Maurice to get it."

"You think it's about money?"

"It usually is."

"But still."

He wasn't convinced. I shrugged again. I thought it was more likely about money than anything else.

Oh boy, how wrong was I?

Stix drained his coffee, fished out some loose change to cover the bill and looked at me.

"So?" He grinned. "What's the plan, boss?"

"You do drive, don't you?" I asked, putting the horse somewhat behind the cart.

"Of course. The bike's just for speed," he said. "And for fun. My rider's Ian Hanratty. He's an ex-racer. Supersport. Not a factory rider, a privateer and a good one. He ran out of money the day before he ran out of brake pads. He works for me now. The hours are shit but the pay's good. Makes more in a week with me than he made in a month at the track."

When I outlined my plan, Stix sat back and looked pleased because it meant he was getting one up on the rest of the paparazzi.

And one up on the cops as well.

I needed to get to the parking lot to retrieve the Mercedes. My foot throbbed and I didn't want to walk. Stix suggested I get a ride with Hanratty. He called him on his mobile and had a few quick words.

"Sorted," he said. "He'll be here in a few minutes. Do you ride?"

"Honda. Blackbird. I've done a few track days too," I added, giving myself a little street cred.

"Yeah? Well, don't tell Hanratty. He'll only show off."

I gave Stix the keys to the four-wheeled block of cheese at the Hertz office, we shook hands, and he left.

By the time I'd finished my coffee, Hanratty was waiting outside.

We fitted the binder into one of the bike's panniers and I slipped the crash helmet over my head, trying hard not to scrape the stitches. I stepped over the bike and grabbed the handrails. I wasn't about to sit backwards.

Hanratty took off smoothly, flowing around the traffic northbound down St. Peter's Street towards the roundabout. I thought it prudent to mention that the police were following us.

"Oh, fuck 'em!" he yelled. "Hang on!"

He got one hell of a lean angle going around the traffic circle and I worried about the tires losing their grip on the wet asphalt. If it worried Hanratty, he didn't show it.

Not one bit.

He gunned it away from the roundabout, heading north, and began a series of cutbacks through countless side streets. I was sure we'd lost our tail the moment he peeled away from the roundabout and overtook a line of cars as though they were standing still but I think he was enjoying himself so I let him have his fun.

We reached the end of Sylvia's street and cruised slowly to the parking lot where he let me off. I thanked him, handed him the helmet and retrieved the binder. He pulled away without another word.

The lanky-haired teenager hadn't come back. Probably out scoring dope with my twenty.

I drove the Mercedes slowly up the hill, giving the paparazzi sufficient time to turn and follow me. We made a strange-looking procession: a dozen cars and the unmarked cruiser that had returned, empty-handed, its antennae between its tail pipes.

They followed me through the town and around Chequer Street, the area I'd chosen as the perfect spot to lose them. Without warning, I turned the Mercedes down a narrow alleyway that ran between two tall buildings. There was barely six inches either side of the car. I drove almost to the end. It opened onto a private rectangular parking area for the staff of a nearby store. There was only one other exit. I stopped with the nose of the Mercedes poking into the square. I powered open the sunroof, enjoying the traffic jam that was building rapidly behind me. When the sunroof was fully open, I switched off the motor, tossed the keys under the passenger seat and levered myself up through the opening.

And it would have been a masterful exit if the back of my pants hadn't hooked on the roof latch.

I was pushing hard to exit the sunroof when down came my pants, underwear and all.

The paparazzi had a field day.

As I struggled to regain a sense of decency, the heat from a million flashbulbs practically seared the skin off my naked and fully exposed rear end.

I could imagine tomorrow's headlines already.

DOESN'T KNOW HIS ARSE FROM HIS ELBOW

Stix was waiting for me in the rented Fiat. He watched in amusement as I struggled to get my pants up. I heard the paparazzi scrambling over the top of the Mercedes as I dived, headlong, into the Fiat.

"Go!" I yelled.

The block of cheese rolled forward, Stix laughing at the sight in his driver's mirror. He aimed a camera over his shoulder and kept the shutter on rapid fire as the paparazzi skidded off the hood of the Mercedes and raced along behind us. He made sure they got a good look at him in the driver's seat.

"Priceless," he said. "Abso-fuckin-lutely priceless."

Then he put the pedal to the metal and the cheese trundled towards the main road south to London.

I watched the traffic behind us and after a long ten minutes decided we weren't being followed.

I phoned Hertz and explained about the Mercedes. I told them it had stalled and I probably flooded it. They were very nice about it. They even apologized and promised to send somebody over to pick it up right away.

We drove in silence for the next few miles. I watched the sky above, wondering if it would ever stop raining.

"It rains all the bloody time these days," Stix said, as if reading my mind. "Where you from?"

"Canada."

"No shit."

"Sorry. Most people think we're American. Then, when you tell them you're Canadian, they tell you 'same difference.'"

"You should wear the maple leaf. We like Canadians. Love 'em, actually. We tolerate the Yanks. Ever since the war."

"Which one?"

"Two. We still think we'd 'ave won it without them, see."

"Well, they helped."

"Maybe. So, where're you from?"

"Calgary."

"The eighty-eight Olympics. I was there. Got some great shots of Eddie the Eagle."

"How long have you been a paparazzo?"

"Since I left school. Nearly twenty years. Had a knack for getting shots others couldn't get. Got offered ten thousand quid for a very unflattering shot of one of the Royals back in the early eighties. Quit my job the very next day, never looked back."

"You enjoy it?"

"Love it."

And I think he really did.

"What do you know about Detective Inspector Gerry Newcombe?" I asked him.

"The Newc?" he said. "Whadya wanna know?"

"He seems a bit of a prick," I said, and Stix nodded.

"That ain't the 'alf of it." He swung out to overtake an eighteen-wheeler, thought better of it and tucked back in behind. "You ever heard of Terry Graham Mercer?"

I shook my head.

"'Bout five, six years ago?"

"No." It still didn't ring any bells.

"The Coffin Killer?"

That rang a bell.

"Yes," I said. "He murdered some children. Left them on a beach, if I remember."

"Yeah," Stix said. "It all started one summer, about six years ago. Couple of kids went missing, about a week apart. Little boy around eight and then a girl about nine. They turned up dead. Sexually assaulted, tied up, gagged and put into homemade coffins while they were still alive. Terry Graham Mercer did that. He drilled holes in the lids and dumped them on a beach late at night, right before the tide came in. He murdered nine kids that summer. Gerry Newcombe caught him. A little boy called Timothy Blake had gone missing about five days earlier. He was kid number ten. Newcombe got lucky. Mercer was pulled over for speeding outside Richmond, in south London. Everyone was looking for him. They took him to Richmond nick. Newcombe knew Mercer had dumped Timmy on a beach somewhere. Nailed him in a coffin drilled full of holes so he'd drown. They didn't have very long before the tide came in, maybe an hour. I had a police scanner, followed them down the coast road. Got pictures as they dragged the box up the beach."

He stared out the windshield, lost in the memory. I could tell it wasn't his finest moment.

"They had Mercer in an interview room at Richmond nick. Newcombe sent the guard out to get him a cup of tea.

When Mercer refused to talk to him, Newcombe offered him a cigarette, lit one for himself, then shoved it straight up Mercer's nose. Can you imagine? A burning hot cigarette right up the snout? Threatened to do the same up the other side but Mercer was gutted. Coughed up a confession right there. They got little Timothy out with a minute to spare. Newcombe was a hero. Except to the bigwigs at Scotland Yard. Mercer lawyered up, started yelling abuse. Newcombe said it was self-inflicted, said he musta been trying to commit suicide."

He paused and grinned and I could tell he'd told the story a time or two.

"And they didn't buy it?" I asked.

"Ha! The bigwigs wanted Newcombe's guts. Suspended him. Next morning, a dozen coppers from Richmond nick showed up with unlit cigarettes behind their ears. It was a silent protest, support for Newcombe. It spread across London in a matter of hours, then right across the country. Coppers everywhere sporting cigarettes behind their ears. You should have seen it. I got a picture of six of them, off duty, hanging around a parking lot. Three of them smoking but all six with a spare behind their ear. Lovely shot. Made the front page the next day. It spread further after that. Everyone started wearing one. Housewives, office workers, bus drivers, even villains. Nobody likes child molesters. Nobody. The whole bleedin' country got behind it and the Yard dropped the case against Newcombe. By then, he was everyone's favourite copper. He got called 'Newc' and it stuck. He finally got a promotion. Four years later."

"So. I'm up against a superhero?"

"Yeah. Doubt he's paid for a pint ever since."

We were quiet for a while after that. Stix drove through thickening traffic, ducking down side streets to avoid gridlocks. I'd never seen traffic so dense, so impenetrable.

I'll never complain about Calgary traffic again.

Well, until the next time.

Chapter Twenty

MR. DERICK B. THOMAS lived in a neat apartment, what the Brits call a flat, on the ground floor of a tall, ugly grey concrete building surrounded by other tall, ugly grey buildings. Stix waited in the car while I went to see Mr. Thomas.

He answered the door on the first ring. He was in his seventies, ramrod straight with a military moustache and tortoiseshell bifocals. His teeth were large and symmetrical and his top lip had trouble covering his uppers.

"Eddie Dancer," I said.

We shook hands on his doorstep before he stepped aside and invited me in. He wore a dark grey suit with his regimental tie.

"How soon will you be needing this translation?" he asked.

"Would tomorrow be pushing it?"

"Hmff."

Which could have been yes.

Or it could have been no.

He led the way down a narrow hall. "How long did you say it was?"

"Thirty pages," I said, and he stopped and looked at me.

"In Old Italian?"

"Yes."

"I see."

He started up again and I followed him past the living room, the kitchen and a small bathroom to a room he used as an office. The room was immaculate. I was surprised to see a computer sitting on his desk. I expected something from the Dark Ages.

Like a quill.

We stood facing each other and he held out his hand. I passed him the binder.

He flipped through it carefully.

"Where did you get this?" he asked.

"A man called Eric Glossard gave it to me. It belonged to his wife's great-great-grandfather."

"I know to whom it belonged," he said. "I've already translated it."

I looked at him for a long moment.

"When?"

"A few days ago."

"For Newcombe?" I asked.

"Detective Inspector Newcombe. Yes."

"Does that prevent you from translating it for me?"

"Can I ask why you need it?" Politely.

"The same reason Detective Inspector Newcombe needed it," I said. "It's evidence in a murder case. I'm trying to prove he's locked up the wrong man."

"I doubt he'd do that," he said. "He's a very good detective."

"So am I," I said. "And I know for a fact that Dr. Peter Maurice is innocent."

"The inspector is something of a legend," Derick Thomas said. "It's really not likely he'd arrest the wrong man."

"So prove me wrong," I said. "Give me your translation."

He thought about it for a moment before making his decision.

"Why don't you just wait a minute," he said. "I'll phone the inspector. If he has no objection, I'll print you a copy."

He moved to pass me but I blocked his way.

"I should probably hang on to that, then," I said and took the binder from him.

He was gone maybe ten minutes. More than enough time to download a copy of the translation from his computer to a floppy disk and get the hell out of there.

But that would be a breach of trust, and I take people's trust in me very seriously.

So I sat in an uncomfortably straight-backed chair and studied his study. One wall was covered with his military history. A service plaque on another wall commemorated twenty-one years of service with the United Nations. He had a huge world map covering most of the far wall where I discovered Estonia, Latvia and Lithuania, although someone may have discovered them even before I did.

"I've spoken with the inspector," he said, when he came back. "I told him where you got that from." He pointed to the binder. "He's not very happy about it. Not very happy at all. But it doesn't appear to me that you have broken any law, so I have no grounds on which to refuse you a copy of the translation."

"Thank you," I said, meaning it. "You'll do it even though Detective Newcombe told you not to?"

"It isn't against the law," he said, stiffly.

I think I rather liked him.

He stepped behind his desk and tapped away at the keyboard. Moments later, his printer spat out page after page of translation.

"What do I owe you?" I asked him.

He looked surprised, as though the thought of charging me hadn't occurred to him.

"I don't know," he said. "I've already been paid for it. It's just the cost of the materials. A couple of bob."

Bob? Who the hell's Bob?

"How much did you charge the inspector?" I asked.

"One hundred pounds," he said. "He was in a most dreadful hurry. I had to postpone several other paying jobs," he added, as if he thought that I thought he'd overcharged the inspector.

"How about half then?" I peeled off fifty pounds, laid the money on the desk.

"That's far too much," he said. "I'm happy with a couple of pounds. Five at the most."

"Treat your wife," I said.

"No." He took five pounds and pushed the rest of the money across the desk. "Not that she doesn't deserve a treat but this'll do just nicely." He gathered up the sheets from the printer tray. "I'll get you an envelope," he said.

"Don't worry," I said and patted the sheets into a neat stack. "Did the inspector happen to mention the curse?" I asked him.

"What curse?"

"Some people think the manuscript is cursed."

"Poppycock." He straightened his tie.

"The reason I mentioned it," I said, "is because the last person who translated that is dead. She was murdered. Undoubtedly for this very translation."

"I survived Dunkirk," he said. "Took a Luger off a Kraut officer. I've still got it. And it still works."

"Good." I thought about offering to buy it from him.

"Good luck to you, Mr. Dancer," he said and we shook hands.

"Thank you," I said. "You take care. And make sure you keep all your windows locked."

"Always do."

On the way out, I paused at the bathroom door.

"May I?" I said. "You Brits and your tea."

"Of course."

He moved off into the living room while I used the washroom. I unraveled three feet of toilet paper, tucked the remaining forty-five pounds under it and wound it back up again. I flushed the toilet and rinsed my hands for effect.

We said goodbye again as he closed the front door behind me. I hoped the old German Luger still had sufficient power to put the bad guys on their ass.

I didn't doubt for a moment that Derick B. Thomas did.

Chapter Twenty-One

"THAT DIDN'T TAKE LONG," Stix said.

I watched him tuck a camera inside its case. He saw me watching, and I realized he'd been taking photos of me with Derick Thomas.

"It's what I do," he said.

"I know it is," I said. "And that's fine, as long as nothing gets published before Peter gets released."

"My word."

He looked over at the stack of papers.

"He'd already translated the manuscript," I said. "He ran me off a copy."

He looked at me for a moment.

"He did one for Newcombe?" he said.

I nodded.

"That makes sense," he said. "He'd be the closest translator for Scotland Yard."

"The old boy phoned Inspector Newcombe, just to make sure he wasn't breaking the law."

"Or that you weren't."

"Or that I wasn't," I conceded.

Old soldiers never die, they just — what? Translate two-hundred-year-old bits of paper and try to stay alive.

I couldn't deny the impatient thrill that coursed through me. I finally had something concrete in my hands that might throw some light on eleven vicious murders.

Even though I still couldn't imagine what.

I began reading the translation in the car but all that did was make me carsick.

"Listen," Stix said. "I live in Bloomsbury, about fifteen minutes away. Why don't we stop by my place and you can read it there? Then we can pick up my car."

"Sure."

I stacked the sheets and pushed them inside the binder and tried to sit patiently while the papers burned a hole in my lap. Stix fought the afternoon traffic, cursing the under-powered Fiat every chance he got. He knew the city like the back of his hand and he pointed out places of interest as we drove by.

"Great Ormond Street Hospital down there," he said. "For sick kids."

I nodded. A few minutes later, he pointed to the left.

"British Museum," he said. "Well worth a butchers."

"Well worth a what?"

"A butchers." He glanced across at me. "Butcher's hook," he said. "A look."

Them and their rhyming slang.

"If I ever get the nickel." I said, making up my own slang.

"The what?"

"Nickel and dime. The time."

He rolled his eyes.

We turned down his street a few minutes later, but could only go partway. A work crew had dug an enormously deep hole in the middle of the road, looking for a burst water main that had flooded the street. Barricades blocked the road on either side of the hole. Nine men stood around looking into it.

"Lazy bastards." Stix backed up and drove around the block.

His house, a tidy two-storey with a front veranda, sat across from a park.

"Come and meet the Sprog," he said as we climbed out.

"The what?"

"My daughter."

He turned the key in his front door and I followed him inside.

"Angie!"

A muffled voice answered, and a girl in her early teens appeared at the top of the stairs. She wore a sleeveless white T-shirt and purple shorts. The youth of today feel neither heat nor cold.

"The bloody water's been off all bloody day, Dad," she complained loudly as though it were his fault. "I can't even take a bloody bath. I'm supposed to go to Wendy's tomorrow. Can you drive me to Mum's?"

"Hello to you, too," Stix said. "Eddie, meet Sprog. Sprog, this is Eddie."

"Hello." She sketched a wave. "Well? Can you?"

"I guess I'll have to," he said. "Have you eaten?"

"How could I?" she said, as though water deprivation stopped her from eating.

"I'll make sandwiches," Stix said. "We have to be at the Elephant and Castle by six. I'll drop you at your mum's on the way."

"Thanks, Dad." She puckered him a kiss and blew it down the stairs. "Mayo's okay. None of that smelly cheese. Whole-wheat brown bread. Toasted. No butter. Cottage cheese. No fish. Lettuce is okay but none of that Popeye shit."

I guessed that would be spinach.

"Celery on the side, no tomatoes. And don't cut the bloody crusts off this time. Who'd ya think I am? Bloody royalty?"

Stix sighed.

"Your language is getting worse." He looked dismayed as he turned to me. "Kids?"

I shook my head.

"No."

"Sometimes," he said, "they can be a right fuckin' liability."

While Stix busied himself in the kitchen, I sat down in the living room and removed the translation carefully from the binder. The living room walls were hung with dozens of framed photographs of the rich and famous and the not-so-rich-and-famous, but my attention was focused on the eleven sheets of paper in my lap. Thirty translated down to eleven. A life's work condensed by computer.

Each page was numbered in the top right-hand corner. As I began reading, skimming the strange prose, I tried to imagine the man writing by candlelight, a scratchy quill on parchment paper.

Mesmer clearly had an agenda. He began by revisiting the personal hardships caused him by the French medical establishment and their continued insistence that "animal magnetism" was nothing more than nature's own course — a natural phenomenon that had nothing to do with him. Mesmer described the escalation of events that finally led to the King's intervention. In 1784, Louis XVI appointed not one, but two separate Royal Commissions to investigate Mesmer's claims. The result was a war of words, a flood of opposing pamphlets that criticized Mesmer's techniques and those of the Royal Commissions.

Clearly disillusioned, Mesmer left France, describing his journeys around Europe before finally settling in his native Germany. He withdrew from the world and took solace in Benjamin Franklin's glass harmonica. He spent time with his few remaining friends, eking out the last of his savings.

Then the tone of his manuscript changed as he changed direction.

He revisited the Royal Commission's findings and began to wonder what part the imagination really played in effecting his cures. He wrote about "belief and expectation" and other methods of hypnotic induction that he had been trying. Verbal suggestions, set to the mournful background accompaniment of the glass harmonica, seemed to induce a trancelike state.

In 1806, he travelled to London to visit an ailing friend, but they had a falling-out. He moved on, spending time at a rundown boarding house down the street from Newgate Prison. He prowled London, looking for subjects on whom to test his newfound theories of induction. But with no money to hire them, he was forced to approach the poorest of the poor, many of whom he found sleeping shoulder to shoulder beneath London's bridges, draped over ropes strung beneath the bridge supports. But these were poorly educated people with only a rudimentary grasp of the English language, and Mesmer grew despondent.

Then, one day, his landlady spoke to him about an opportunity at Newgate Prison. The warden held great sway over what went on in Newgate and, for a trifling sum, would release a prisoner into Mesmer's custody.

Intrigued, Mesmer approached the warden. They struck a deal. In return for healing the warden's wife and her sister (of what, he didn't say), Mesmer had his pick of prisoners. Since he had nowhere to take them, the warden offered him a small storeroom at the back of the prison where they kept their provisions.

And it was there, in that cold, dark storeroom in Newgate Prison, that Mesmer had his epiphany. There he met, face to face, the monster unleashed almost two hundred years later. A monster that had been resurrected and had killed eleven people. A monster that had split my head open with his crash helmet.

And it was all there.

In black and white.

For anyone gullible enough to believe it.

Chapter Twenty-Two

"I'LL TRADE YOU," Stix said.

I looked up. He held a plate of sandwiches. I traded them for the translation of the manuscript.

"I'll be in the kitchen," he said.

To take my mind off what I'd read, because I was having a hard time processing it, I wandered around the living room, chewing on white bread sandwiches and looking more closely at Stix's photo gallery. The living room was fairly small, and there was almost no wall space left. There were maybe a hundred framed photographs, half in black and white, the rest in colour. I found the one of the six policemen taking their break with the cigarettes behind their ears. It was a great shot. I recognized a lot of the people in the other photographs. Big names such as Madonna and Paul McCartney, Sean Penn, Tiger Woods and Dave Beckham and a great shot of the Dixie Chicks, huddled under a tiny umbrella while caught in a cloudburst, heads back, laughing hard as water cascaded off them. On the far wall, I saw an overhead shot of Michael Jackson carrying his masked son. His son's face mask had slipped down, and the boy's features were clearly visible.

"That one's not for sale."

I turned. It was Angie, standing in the doorway. "My dad could have got a hundred thousand quid for that picture," she said. "He never sent it in. It was an invasion of privacy. Jacko hates his kids being photographed. Dad says it was a security risk."

"A hundred thousand pounds?" I said.

"Sure. See that one?" She pointed to a picture of Britney Spears falling off a skateboard. It was the one from his web page. "He got twenty grand for that. If he could have got her landing on her arse, he'd have got fifty grand, easy, for the pair."

"Why didn't he?"

"Bodyguards," she said. "They're everywhere. They tried to smash his camera."

"People do that to cameras?" I said.

"All the time," she said.

Imagine that.

On the wall beside the fireplace were his Stones photos. Good, crisp shots and not one of them an easy stage shot. A few on patios, some on beaches, two out on the water, maybe the Caribbean. A close-up of Charlie looking ill, climbing down from a hot-air balloon.

But the pièce de résistance was a full colour photograph of the four Stones, Mick, Keith, Charlie and Ronnie, sitting astride colourful children's tricycles, racing towards an imaginary finish line. They were all laughing, all bunched close together crashing into one another, all having the time of their lives. Great mates with not a care in the world. They wore the most amazing array of primary colours, hats and silk scarves, jackets and shirts, tight pants and boots. The camera caught every piece of jewelry, every trinket in Keith's hair, every crease in Mick's face.

But best of all were their signatures. And they'd personalized them to Stix. It was a great shot and one I'd never seen before.

Why would I?

The reason they had signed it for him was they trusted him not to sell it to the highest bidder.

"Are you a fan?" she said.

"Yeah," I told her. "I first saw them live in Edmonton. The Bridges to Babylon tour. Then again in Calgary when they played the Saddledome. The biggest concert Calgary's ever seen."

"My dad channels Keith," she said, proudly.

"You don't say."

I didn't tell her you had to be dead to be channelled.

Stix and Stones.

"How d'you know my dad?" she asked.

"He kept trying to take my photograph."

"Are you famous?" she asked.

"Infamous," I said.

"What's the difference?"

I looked around at the pictures on the walls.

"About twenty-five thousand quid." I said. "Do you study photography?"

"No. I study art. I love drawing. That's what I want to do when I grow up."

I had a sudden, crazy idea.

"Can you sketch me someone I saw? I only caught a glimpse."

"You want like an Identikit picture, you mean?"

"A what?"

"Like the police use. When they have a witness."

"Yes. Can you do that?"

She shrugged.

"I'll try."

I described my assailant to Angie as best I could. She used a piece of charcoal and a sketch pad. I described his face and she fleshed out his eyes, nose and lips using her thumb to smudge the lines. It took about ten minutes but the resemblance was actually very good, given what she had to work with.

"I'll pay you," I offered.

"Don't be daft." She tore it off the pad. "I'm not that good, yet. Do you want me to sign it?"

"Better not," I said.

I didn't want her name anywhere near it. She put her pad and charcoals away.

"Well, it was nice meeting you." She smiled at me. "I've got to pack a few things before we go."

I finished my sandwich and took another tour of the room. I was looking at the Dixie Chicks again when Stix came back.

"Jesus H. Christ, Eddie." He waved the translation. "What a freakin' story this is turning out to be."

"Only if you believe it," I said.

"What's not to believe?" he said. "It's all there!"

"It proves nothing, Stix. Except that some wacko got hold of the manuscript and turned it into a self-fulfilling prophecy."

"How could he? It's been up in that attic for two hundred years," he said. "You said so yourself."

"Since then, I mean. Since the Glossards found it, someone got hold of it, translated it and now they think they're the devil reincarnate."

"I don't buy that," he said emphatically.

"Well, I don't buy the other," I said. "It's all mumbo-jumbo, claptrap."

"Tell that to the dead women," he said.

And for the first time, I had no clever comeback.

Chapter Twenty-Three

MESMER'S MANUSCRIPT, PAGES 24 through 30.

A foul day. Fog hangs thick like lichen. Muffled coughing everywhere. I sleep poorly. Damp shoes. My bones ache. I walk around Newgate, one hand to the wall, fearing losing my way.

The Warden's mood is fouler than the weather today, angry with Thomas Simmons, my new patient. They will start to put him to death today. I plead for a day so I may finish. I pledge further sessions with his wife, her sister.

"Perhaps," the Warden promises.

The room is cold. Thomas knows he is to die. He is difficult. We are losing time. I watch his breathing. When it slows, I hold him with a gaze. He watches, scared but calmer. I speak the words and watch his eyes. They close. I talk again, counting. His head drops. His body slumps. He is magnetized.

I tell him, "Speak your name."

"Thomas Simmons."

He speaks slowly, as if in slumber.

And then I know that he is ready.

"Go forth," I tell him, and such is my excitement, "go forth again to your next time of being."

And he breathes a great shudder as his head rolls. He sits straight now. I wait while he moves through time, then command him: open the eyes! He looks not at me but across the room, as if walls do not exist. He looks through them to a great distance. Not miles, but a great distance in time.

"Where are you now?" I ask him.

"London," he says.

"And how far have you travelled there?"

And he answers: "Quite two hundred years."

"What work do you do in this London?"

"My work," he answers.

"Which is?" I say and he answers.

"I crush women who vex me."

"In London?" I ask and he says:

"And south."

I ask how many and he says, "Many."

"More than fingers on your hand?" I ask.

"Aye," he says, "many more than they."

But the Warden speaks not the truth to me. For they came then and took Thomas Simmons to begin his death. Not the quickness of the hanging or drawing and quartering but the awful slow death beneath the door. I knew of the courtyard, of the chains in the floor and watched them beat him down and fasten him, wide of limb. Four guards to the door. They took it from his cell, a heavy blackened oak slab with iron hinges, and they put it on him. I begged for him but they said they would put the wood to him and shewed me the triangles they would put beneath him if I pleaded more.

But they let me be there.

And on the door, a new rock every day. The heaviness never quite enough to crush his life completely. They gave him water, some gruel. Ten days passed. And ten rocks. He breathed so hard, his voice raw from his screams. He begged my help. All day. At last, I brought someone. A heavy man from the street. When the guards looked away, we climbed on the rocks on the door. Minutes passed. I heard his fragile ribs break above his screams. He begged us off but I gave him my promise. I know not when he passed. His breath sounds gave my friend feint of heart and I paid again to have him stay. His breaths, at last, had slowed.

And stopped.

I left and wept for him.

May God have mercy on his soul.

And all those before him.

And those still yet to come.

Franz-Anton Mesmer
1807

So there it was.

The final six pages of a two-hundred-year-old manuscript — the reason a dozen people had been murdered, their heads slowly crushed beyond recognition.

While today's hypnotists regress their subjects back to past lives, Mesmer had progressed his to a future one. He had hypnotized a prisoner in Newgate and sent him forward, almost two hundred years into the future, to share with him the details of his next life, the life of a modern-day serial killer. A man who killed women who vexed him by crushing their heads. And his death count was greater than the number of fingers on both his hands.

I had read it twice.

But I still didn't believe a word of it.

But, dammit, neither did I believe in coincidence.

Chapter Twenty-Four

WE LEFT THE FIAT AND rode in Stix's car, an immaculate, four-door silver Jaguar. Angie climbed in the back with her suitcase and I rode shotgun. I was surprised how little legroom there was. That wasn't a design fault, it was all the electronic gear Stix had hard-wired into the car. There was a police scanner, global positioning equipment, a fax machine, two-way radio and a laptop with a modem. The rest was beyond my comprehension.

"Sorry." Stix nodded towards the abundance of equipment. "My office away from home."

By mutual agreement, neither of us discussed Mesmer or Newgate Prison in front of Angie.

As we got under way, Angie asked about my life in Calgary.

She thought it was really funny that we often plug in our cars during winter. She asked if we were close to the mountains. I told her we were and talked about everything from skiing and ice fishing to making snow angels and riding mountain bike trails. I told her about the glacial lakes, the amazing scenery and the incredible wildlife.

"Have you ever seen a wild bear?"

So I told her all the bear stories I'd ever heard and some I hadn't and when I finished she declared that Canada was her most favourite place in the world and she'd give anything to go there for a holiday.

"Could I stay with you?" she asked and, in an unguarded moment, I said maybe she could.

We detoured across London to Bayswater, on the west side, where Stix's ex-wife, Sharon, worked at an old-fashioned hotel with a lively bar in the basement. She was the night manager and she also booked the stand-up comics, rock bands and solo artists. She was behind the counter, on the phone, arguing with a band manager, when we arrived. Sharon listened to the manager for a few more seconds before hanging up on him in mid-sentence.

"Jerk." She looked at Stix. "Speaking of which, what do you want?"

"The water's off. Sprog needs a bath."

The woman lifted the counter flap and Angie walked through.

"Hi, Mum."

They air kissed and Angie said goodbye to us both before she disappeared behind a door marked Private. Stix's ex-wife turned to him.

"Can't you pay the sodding water bill?" she snarled.

"It's a burst main," Stix said, not wanting to get into it with her.

"What sort of a life is it for her? You traipsing around, taking snapshots, her stuck indoors, can't even get a bleedin' bath." She turned to me. "Who are you?"

"Donald Trump," I said, extending my hand towards her, but she ignored it. "I'm buying up hotels in Bayswater."

"Trump?"

"You've heard of me?" I said.

"Who bleedin' hasn't," she said. "Why'd you wanna buy this dump?"

"To knock it down."

"What about me?" she demanded.

"You're fired," I said.

"Bleedin' 'ell!" She looked like she was going to come over the counter at me. "You bleedin' Yanks. Who do you bleedin' well think you are?"

"Now you see why Sharon's my ex, Donald," Stix said. "Come on, let's go."

I followed him out of the hotel and we climbed into the Jag.

"She has a mouth on her," Stix apologized. "Never knew when to keep a civil tongue in her head. Still doesn't."

When we were back into the late afternoon traffic, I brought the conversation round to Mesmer.

"We need to find a link," I told him.

"What sorta link?"

"Between Mesmer and Newgate Prison. One that proves that other people knew about his experiments with Thomas Simmons." A link, in other words, that would put an end to the reincarnation nonsense. "So where is Newgate Prison?" I asked.

"It burnt down years ago. Horrible place. Nobody wanted anything to do with it, that's why it was never rebuilt."

"There'll be records, though."

"Sure. But here's a question. How did this bloke that's killed all these women know your doctor friend had been in touch with Maria Glossard?"

"I don't know."

"How did he know Gina Lansdale had a copy of the manuscript?"

"I don't know that, either."

"And how did he know you had an appointment to see her?"

"I wish I knew."

"So how did he know your doctor friend was out of the nick when he murdered Gina Lansdale?"

"I don't know that, either."

"You're not much of a fuckin' detective then, are you?"

That had an alarming ring of truth about it.

"There's a bloke I know in New York," he said. "Danny Falco, runs a research company. If you've read any best-sellers in the last ten years, chances are, Danny's company did some of the research for the author. He's mainly a writer's source but I've used him lots of times. He's bloody good and bloody fast. And bloody expensive. But he owes me on account I send him a lot of business."

"How do we get hold of him?"

"That's easy."

He pulled over and parked near a corner, got honked at and ignored it. He reached across the car and pulled a slim laptop from the holster near my right leg. He flipped up the monitor and booted up the computer. He opened his email program. He was a hunt-and-peck guy like me, cursing every time he missed a key. Which was often.

"How's that?"

I read the message.

DANNY — NEED LINK BETWEEN DOCTOR FRANZ-ANTON MESMER (DIED 1815) AND NEWGATE PRISON, LONDON. SPECIFICALLY NEED DOCUMENTATION OF MESMER'S USE OF PRISONERS FOR HYPNOTIC EXPERIMENTS. HIGHEST PRIORITY. STIX.

"When will he get it?"

Stix hit the send key and looked at his watch.

"About now," he said.

"I mean, it's probably midnight in New York."

"He's open twenty-four, seven. Has a huge staff of researchers online all over the world. He'll probably send it to a bunch of staffers here in London. We should hear back in an hour or two."

I was impressed.

"Remind me to get his email address from you."

He pulled into traffic.

"By the way," he said. "Are you planning on telling me why we are going to the Elephant and Castle?"

"I have to meet somebody."

"No shit?"

"You're better off not knowing."

"It's illegal?"

"So I'm told."

"And you're not going to tell me?"

"I'll tell you afterwards."

"After what?"
"After I meet the guy."
"I thought we were partners."
"Think of it more as a master-slave relationship," I said.
"Which am I?"
Before I could answer, my cell phone rang.
"Change of venue," the man's distorted voice said.
"Hang on," I said, "talk to my slave."
I handed the phone to Stix.

Chapter Twenty-Five

STIX HUNG UP AND HANDED me the phone.

"We're going to Dockland," Stix said. "The Dog and Duck. It's a pretty mean area. Lots of hard men live down the docks. The D & D's a real rough pub."

"You know where it is?"

"Oh yeah. I know where it is."

We drove in silence and I could understand why he was pissed at me. But what he didn't know couldn't hurt him. We drove down darkened streets, the uneven cobblestones pounding the Jag's suspension. The houses got closer together and we passed row upon row of terraced homes. A poor man's Coronation Street. The farther we drove, the more dismal the scenery. Even the air smelled bad. Stix pulled up across the street, finally, from a derelict-looking brick building with an illegible sign that might have said Dog and Duck.

Or it might have said Go Away. Visitors Not Welcome.

"You want me to come with you?" Stix asked.

"They never said come alone," I told him.

We climbed from the car and I hung my raincoat from my shoulders, a theatrical gesture but that's what the man on the phone had told me to do. As we turned to cross the street, a gang of kids came over to us, none over the age of twelve. The ringleader stood maybe four feet tall, a shock of black, curly hair and face full of freckles. A lit cigarette hung from the corner of his mouth.

"Tenner to watch the motor, guv," he told Stix.

Stix pulled out a ten-pound note, tore it in half and handed half to the curly-haired kid who folded it once and tucked it in his pocket.

"Snitch." The kid summoned one of the other boys, a lad about eight with a runny nose and grubby knees. "He's your minder," he said. "Can he sit inside? He's got a rotten cold."

Stix opened the back door for him.

"Touch anything, I'll chop your fingers off," Stix told Snitch.

"I won't," Snitch said, sounding full of the flu.

Stix locked him in the car. We walked across the street to the Dog and Duck.

"Bit risky," I said.

"No, it's not. They could break in in thirty seconds, take everything they want and be gone in under a minute. This way, they respect you. He won't touch anything. It's bad for business. And if he did, it wouldn't be me chopping off his fingers."

I moved ahead and we pushed our way into the dingy clamour of the Dog and Duck.

As pubs go, it wasn't the filthiest pub in Great Britain.

But it was in the top two.

The place was three-quarters full. Most of the drinkers were men who sat around tables nursing pints of beer. Cigarette smoke clung to the ceiling in a thick haze. There was no piano, no stand-up comic doing his shtick, no band of girl singers putting it out front. The conversations were muted. This was a pub for serious drinkers.

A joyless place.

The end of the line.

We endured outright hostility as we worked our way to the bar and ordered two pints of draft, then I went to the door and hung up my coat, as per the telephone instructions. I was not to look at it for twenty minutes. We sat at the bar with our backs to the coat rack while I watched my coat's reflection in the mirror behind the bar. Midway through the first pint, it was still there.

It was warm in the bar and Stix took off his coat, laying it across his lap. He was wearing a short-sleeved shirt and I noticed the bottom half of an odd looking tattoo on his bicep.

"What's that?" He hiked up his shirtsleeve and revealed what looked like a bar code.

"Fosters Lager," he said and laughed. "Had it done with a bunch of Aussies a few years back."

"Does it scan?"

He shook his head.

"No, but I've had more Fosters bought for me than I've paid for."

I glanced in the mirror and saw my coat was missing, along with the three hundred and fifty pounds in the inside pocket. I hoped I could trust the man on the phone.

Oh well, any friend of Nosher's.

As Stix turned to his drink, a big man with a huge barrel chest and hairy great forearms nudged him.

"What's all that shit in your hair, then?" The man leaned in as he spoke and we could both smell the beer on his breath.

"Souvenirs," Stix said, affecting a slight lisp. "One for every blow job. I've got loads of 'em. Got room for one more, if you think you're man enough."

The man blinked, like he didn't quite get it. Then he did, and didn't like it. He backed up a foot, getting very red in the face. His pouty bottom lip stuck out beyond his chin line.

"You fuckin' faggot! I'm gonna shove your fuckin' head up your arse!"

I moved in between them.

"You're just supposed to create a mild diversion," I told him. "Not World War Three." I glanced across the room in time to see a woman with flaming red hair hang my coat up. "My coat's back now so we don't need a scene, all right?"

He stopped and looked at me, unsure who I was. Then he stuck out his bottom lip even further, going for petulant, and prodded me hard with a fat, dirty fingernail.

"Fuck off, you pansy Yank!"

He turned to Stix and grabbed him by the throat. I reached across and got my nails in his protruding bottom lip. I gave it a hard, sharp twist. His head tilted to one side and he grimaced in pain.

But he let go of Stix's throat.

A few of the old-timers took their beer and moved away.

"I'm not a pansy Yank," I told him, "I'm a pansy Canadian." I tweaked his lip even harder, driving him down to one knee. "So get it right."

I think he said something rude.

I whispered in his ear.

"Now that I've got a gun," I said, "don't make me shoot you."

And then all hell broke loose. Which was something I didn't know about English pubs. Well, workingmen's pubs, anyway. They are just a single punch away from total anarchy. Before I could let go of his lip, someone grabbed me from behind and tried to tear my head off. Next came the sound of breaking glass, of tables overturned, of fists hitting flesh and bone hitting bone.

I brought my elbow back into somebody's solar plexus and heard a grunt near my left ear as my assailant doubled. The barrel-chested goon stood and reached for a bar stool just as Stix threw the remains of a beer in his face then punched him hard in the nose.

All around me, the room erupted in a dozen separate brawls. Brave men went toe-to-toe, trading solid body punches. The less brave broke beer bottles and stabbed anyone not bright enough to keep their distance.

Shortened pool cues appeared and cracked heads and collarbones. Handfuls of loose change became weapons of mass destruction, curled into fists to make solid contact or flung across the room as sharpened missiles.

I saw the barman reach under the bar and come up with a shillelagh, a polished wooden cudgel favoured by the fighting Irish. He swung it hard at several nearby fighters and I grabbed Stix in time to save him a nasty crack upside the head.

"Be a good time to leave," I said.

"Hairy bastard." Stix kicked the barrel-chested goon in the groin.

I grabbed Stix by the collar and dragged him behind me. The floor was a sea of brawling arms and legs, upturned chairs and tables and broken bottles. I made my way between them, warding off the most aggressive before they could level me.

There was no rhyme or reason to any of it. Brother attacked brother, neighbour attacked neighbour, friend attacked friend. It was just what they did. Pent-up aggression, some ill-perceived slight from days, weeks or even years gone by. It all came to the surface in one big brawl.

I reached the rack, grabbed my coat and hauled Stix backwards through the door and onto the street. The noise inside was deafening and I was glad of the respite as we stood on the pavement outside.

"Jesus!" Stix said.

He was looking at me with great concern.

"What's the matter?" But I knew what he was going to say.

"Your head's bleeding!"

I reached up and felt my stitches. They had come loose in the brawl, and fresh blood gushed down my cheek.

"It'll keep," I said. I patted my pockets, felt something heavy in the pocket. "Let's go."

As we turned to cross the street, the door behind us opened and the redhead stepped out.

"'Ello, darlin'." She stumbled into me and as she did so, she took something from her pocket. "Smile, lover."

She pointed a camera at my face, blinding me with the flash.

"Cheese," I said.

"Make my boyfriend jealous," she said and patted my cheek. The unbloodied side.

She turned and walked quickly away, not drunk at all.

"What was that all about?" Stix asked.

"Insurance," I said. "Don't worry about it."

We crossed to the car and Stix let Snitch out the back of the Jag. He gave him the other half of the ten-pound note.

"Ta." Snitch wiped his nose on his sleeve. "Nice motor."

We climbed into the nice motor and Stix fired it up but he didn't put it in gear.

"Show me," he said.

"Show you what?"

"What you just bought."

I dropped the SIG Sauer into his outstretched hand.

"I can't be unarmed," I told him. "I'll understand if you disapprove."

He turned the gun over, studied it a moment before handing it back.

"I figured you more as a Smith and Wesson kinda guy," he said. "Lock it in the glovebox." He put the car in gear and pulled away from the curb. "You ever shoot anyone?"

"Yes."

"Ever kill 'em?"

"That's rather the point of shooting them, isn't it?"

Neither of us said very much after that.

Chapter Twenty-Six

STIX SPUN THE LAPTOP around on the café tabletop and I read the email that had arrived from Danny Falco. We'd stopped by a drugstore and bought a box of plasters and some gauze so I could clean myself up and tape my damaged eyebrow shut. Now we were sitting in a greasy spoon ordering tea on our way back across London. I adjusted the laptop screen to block out the overhead light and read the message.

STIX. NO CONNECTION MESMER/NEWGATE PRISON. NOTHING. ZERO. ZILCH. WEB LINKS BOTH PARTIES ATTACHED FYI. DANNY.

There were two attachments that gave a list of separate web pages, one dedicated to Dr. Franz-Anton Mesmer and the other to Newgate Prison. The Mesmer links were ones I'd already checked out myself. At the bottom of the Newgate list, Danny Falco had added a postscript that read:

RONALD VARNEY, LUTON, BEDFORDSHIRE, ENGLAND. GUY'S A NEWGATE NUT. BEST UNOFFICIAL COLLECTION OF NEWGATE MEMORABILIA ANYWHERE. NO WEB PAGE OR EMAIL. LEFT

PHONE MESSAGE. NO REPLY. CALL HIM DIRECT FOR MORE INFO.

Danny Falco had included Ronald Varney's home phone number and his street address.

"Hmm."

I turned the laptop towards Stix.

"Hmm?"

"Here's the problem." I stirred my tea. I wanted to make sure Stix and I were both on the same page. I also wanted to make sure I wasn't missing anything. "The Glossards bring the manuscript to England to sell it. Supposedly, they don't tell a soul about it. Nobody. They track down Peter Maurice and negotiate a price. Peter tells his wife, Sylvia, but no one else. Not even his publisher, okay?"

He looked at me like he was about to object.

"Go along for the moment," I said.

"All right."

"Okay." I continued. "After Maria mails the manuscript to Peter, she gets murdered. Then nine more women get murdered in much the same way. The police intercept the manuscript, decide they've got their hands on a major clue. Won't discuss it. In fact, won't even admit it exists. I get a copy, give it to Geoffrey Lansdale so his wife can translate it. His wife gets murdered and the copy and the translation are stolen. We get the second copy translated and it sort of suggests a serial killer might be at large, crushing women's heads. But apart from the manuscript, we can find no other material linking Mesmer to Newgate Prison."

"So?"

"So, here's the problem." I took a sip of tea. "Whoever is doing the killings has already read the manuscript. He's fashioned his M.O. on the translation."

"But you said nobody knows about it," Stix countered, scoring a point for the Brotherhood of Reincarnated Souls.

"Nobody I *know* knows about it," I said. "We can make one of two assumptions." I counted them off on my fingers. "One. Nobody knew about the manuscript until Eric Glossard found it. Someone read it after he found it. Or two, somebody else found the manuscript before Eric Glossard did, read it, put it back where they found it, then killed Maria when they realized she was going to sell it."

"But why? Why put it back?"

"My point, exactly. If somebody found it, then why put it back? Why go to all the trouble of resealing the knot with wax? If it's so incriminating, why not just destroy it?" I shook my head. "I think we can discount that idea. Nobody found it before Eric Glossard. I think it's been read since it arrived in England."

"But how? And by whom?"

"If I knew that, I could go home."

We sat and supped our teas, waiting for inspiration. I knew there were still avenues to explore, but I was still curious about Newgate Prison.

A prison that no longer existed.

"Where's Luton?" I asked. It was where Ronald Varney lived.

"North." Stix drained his tea. "Half hour from St. Albans."

"Fancy a drive?"

"If he's home."

I picked up my cell phone and dialed Ronald Varney's

home number. After a slight pause, it began to ring, a distinctive double-warbling tone.

"'Ello?"

A gruff, male voice.

"Mr. Varney?"

"Yeah?"

"My name's Eddie Dancer, Mr. Varney. I got your number from a man named Danny Falco in New York."

"Yeah?"

"I understand you're an expert on Newgate Prison."

"Yeah?"

It was like pulling teeth.

"And, if that's the case, I wonder if I might talk with you about it?"

"Yeah?"

"You are a Newgate expert, are you?"

"Who are you again?"

"Eddie Dancer."

"Where you callin' from?"

"London."

"You said New York."

"That's where Danny Falco lives. He gave me your number."

"Never 'eard of 'im," he said.

"Nonetheless," I said, patiently, "he knows of you, Mr. Varney."

"Well, it's more'n just an 'obby."

"A what?"

"An 'obby."

"Right. A hobby."

"S'more'n that." He was indignant. I was wishing I'd let Stix make the call.

"Of course," I soothed him. "I'm looking for information about a particular prisoner."

"That'll cost ya."

"I'm willing to pay," I said. "But I need to know if you can help me."

"Course. I've got the names of all of them what was imprisoned. What year?"

"Early eighteen hundreds," I said.

"Yeah."

"Can I come by tonight?"

"Tonight?"

"If that's convenient."

"Yeah, all right. I'm not going nowhere."

I confirmed his address and Stix estimated we'd be there in an hour and a half.

Luton's a blue-collar town with a heavy ethnic mix. We took the M1 motorway and turned at the first Luton exit. We drove down dark streets looking for Ronald Varney's house. He lived in what the Brits call a semi-detached bungalow and what Calgarians call a side-by-side duplex. He lived in the left-hand half and I could see his neighbour was anything but house-proud. Varney's side was freshly painted, the outside stucco glowing white with a vertical line separating his paintwork from the neighbouring house, which looked shabby, its front yard overgrown, the drapes at the windows threadbare and badly hung. We parked behind a dark blue Ford van and Stix locked the Jag and tripped the alarm.

"Can't be too careful," he said.

I rang the bell and we listened to the chimes roll through the house. A light came on in the hall and a small woman with powder-grey hair opened the front door.

"Yes?" She was a brusque, no-nonsense lady in her mid-sixties. She glanced at my homemade bandage job but said nothing.

"I've an appointment with Mr. Varney," I said. "Eddie Dancer. And this is . . ." I forgot his real name.

"Stix." He reached out and shook hands with the elderly lady. "He's from Canada," he said, as though pardoning an indiscretion.

"Come in." She stood aside. "I'll put the kettle on, shall I?"

"Aye." Stix rubbed his hands together, relishing yet another cup of tea. I wondered where they put it all.

"Ronnie's in the lav," she said. "Come on."

I thought she said "lab" and imagined a laboratory with rats and a maze but then I heard the toilet flush and realized she'd said "lav." Ronald Varney came out a little quicker than he would if he'd bothered to wash his hands.

I should have realized, when I saw the acres of lino throughout the place and the custom enlarged doorframes, that Ronald Varney was in a wheelchair. He rolled down the hallway towards us.

"Mr. Dancer's here," his wife said.

"Put kettle on, then."

She smiled at me as if to say, "Don't mind him," and steered us into the back room, Ronald Varney's shrine to Newgate Prison. He followed us in.

"It gives me the willies," his wife said, ignoring Ronald as she rubbed her shoulders, "but it keeps him outta my hair. He's been a right bloody nuisance since he retired."

"Right, then." Ronald ignored her and swung his wheelchair around to face us. "Holy crap! What happened to your 'ead?"

"A crash helmet fell on it," I said.

"From a bloody great height, by the look of it," he said. "All right." He looked from one to the other of us. "Who's which?"

"Eddie." I pointed at my chest. "Stix." I pointed to Stix.

"'Ello," he said.

He didn't offer to shake hands.

Thank God for small mercies.

His office, like the prison itself, was a dark place. Two rooms knocked into one. It was full of filing cabinets and there were detailed charts on the walls. A black-and-white blow-up of Newgate Prison was pinned to the wall opposite the door. A desk was jammed tightly between a photocopier and a tall brown filing cabinet. There was one narrow chesterfield between two filing cabinets.

I wedged myself in next to Stix.

"So, whatcha wanna know?" Ronnie asked.

"Give me some background," I said. "Two minutes about the prison itself."

He sat back, rubbed two-day-old stubble with cigarette-stained fingers. A pair of bifocals sat high in his thinning grey hair. His eyes were weak, washed out from the blue of his youth. He wore a dirty yellow cardigan over a white shirt, buttoned to the collar without a tie, like the man in the ING commercial.

"Well." He scratched himself. "It were demolished in

nineteen-oh-four. Good riddance, too. It were a grim place and no mistake. It'd been a prison since the beginning of the twelfth century. It were actually London's fifth Gatehouse but they turned it into a prison. It were only s'posed to hold a hundred or so but they used to fill it up with nearly three hundred poor souls most all the time. It were a mixed prison, too. Men, women, kids. Didn't matter if they'd been to trial or not, they all got lumped together. It weren't run as a reformatory, just a place to hold them poor buggers awaiting trial. After they'd been convicted, they were brought back to Newgate for their sentence to be carried out. The lucky buggers got shipped off to the colonies. Others — murderers, thieves, forgers — they got hung. Some got hung, drawn and quartered. Hanging was bad enough, mind. Didn't drop them off a scaffold and break their necks quick like. Just shoved them off a little handcart. Their families would hang from their legs, try and make it quicker for them, the poor bastards."

Mrs. Varney came in with the tea tray, then left, and we all helped ourselves. Ronald rolled a cigarette with tobacco from a worn Old Holborn tin. He licked the edge of the paper, then ran the freshly rolled cigarette between his lips to dampen it so it wouldn't burn down too quickly.

"So, who d'you wanna know about?" he asked me as he lit the cigarette from a wooden match.

"His name was Thomas Simmons," I said. "He'd have been there around eighteen-oh-seven. Give or take a year."

Ronald Varney took a deep drag, put the burning roll-up in the ashtray and turned to one of his many filing cabinets. "Simmons, you said."

"Yes."

I watched him work one of the middle drawers open. He leaned over and riffled slowly through a pack of tightly stored files. He worked one out from near the middle.

"Simmons," he read the file tag. "T. Simmons." He looked at me with suspicion. "You said his name was Thomas?"

"Yes."

"How would you know that?"

"I read it."

"Read it where?"

"In an old manuscript." Which was all I was prepared to tell him at that point.

"Been my life's work, collecting all this." He placed a hand atop the filing cabinet. "Sometimes, it's hard to get the full name. Prison records weren't always that good. I've never been able to find Simmons's first name. You say you read it?"

"Yes."

"What manuscript might that be, then?"

"I'm not at liberty to say. Not right now." I softened it for him. "But I might be able to let you have a copy, if all goes well."

"If all what goes well?"

"If you scratch my back while I'm scratching yours," I told him.

He thought about that for a while.

"We'll see," he said, laying the file folder on the desk behind him. Out of reach. "What's your interest in Simmons?"

"I don't know," I told him. "I'm working for a client who's been accused of something he didn't do. One thing led to another which led me to you."

"What client?"

I shook my head.

"Tell you what," he said. "I'll let you read my file, you let me read yours."

"No." I shook my head. "It doesn't belong to me."

"Who does it belong to?" he fired back.

"My client."

"Feck," he cursed under his breath. "How do I know you'll keep your word?"

"You don't," I told him.

"So why should I help you?"

Stix and I stood up together.

"Thanks for your time, Mr. Varney," I said.

We started to leave but he wheeled his chair quickly across the room and stopped us.

"Don't go getting' the hump," he said. "We can work summat out."

Stix and I exchanged a shrug.

We sat down.

"If I show you that —" he pointed to the file "— will you at least promise to try and get me the stuff you read?"

I put my hand over my heart and promised. He reached out and picked up Simmons's file and handed it over without another word.

I rested it on my lap and opened it. Stix looked over my shoulder. The first page was a copy of something headed the Newgate Calendar. It was dated 7 March 1808 and comprised three separate columns. The first was a list of the names of prisoners scheduled for trial at the Old Bailey. About a quarter of the way down the list, Ronnie had highlighted the name T. Simmons in yellow marker. The second column listed their offences. I glanced down the row. The offences ranged from High Treason to Forgery but most were Murder. Against T. Simmons's name it said: "The man of Blood, Murder, Hertford."

I didn't know what Hertford was.

"Who did he murder?"

"Next page," he said.

The second page contained a handwritten account of Simmons's crime. He had murdered his wife. In his defence, he claimed she was having an affair with a neighbour. He had dragged her out of bed early one morning, beat her in the kitchen and then stepped on her hair, pinning her head to the floor. He had placed a heavy rock on the kitchen table earlier. He dropped the rock on her head, repeatedly, until she was dead. There was a tremendous amount of blood. He showed no remorse at trial. He was sentenced to death, the sentence to be carried out within ten days. The prosecution used the presence of the rock to argue premeditation. There were three prior murders, all with similar M.O.s. All of them young women known to Simmons, but the prosecution only had sufficient evidence that he had murdered his wife and didn't lay any additional charges.

The second page was headed The Ordinary of Newgate.

"What's an ordinary?" I asked Varney.

"The chaplain," he said. He leaned back in his chair and

steepled his fingers. "Around that time, the chaplain of Newgate began publishing accounts of each prisoner's trial and their punishment. Each account was divided into five parts." He counted them off on his fingers. "First, the trial itself. Then any Biblical quotes he used to preach to the condemned prisoner. Then a bit of a biography about the prisoner's life, often including a bit supposedly written by the condemned himself. Then a bit about the actual type of offence, the legal description, so to speak, then the execution and how they handled themselves. That part was very popular." He chuckled.

The third page, the last page in the file, was empty except for the handwritten notation Not B.C.

"What does that mean?" I turned the file to face him but he already knew what I was going to ask him.

"B.C. stands for Blood Code. Back then, they really liked to see lots of blood. Most executions were public affairs. Hangings were sometimes not enough for the crowd. If the condemned had somehow displeased them, the crowd might call for his blood. Or hers. Then they'd be drawn and quartered. They'd cut them open, two big cuts like a cross over their stomach, like so." He drew a cross low on his stomach. "Then they'd pull their guts out. They were supposed to hang them first but hanging didn't guarantee they were dead. Sometimes they'd tie them to four different horses. A limb apiece. They'd whip the horses and the horses would tear them apart. Other times, they'd hang them and burn them. Or they just burned them alive. That's what the Blood Code was all about. The more blood, the better."

"So what does No Blood Code mean?"

"The warden had leeway." Varney was just warming up. He leant forward and rested his arms on top of his thighs. "If a prisoner got the warden mad or upset his jailers, the warden had the power to choose how the prisoner died."

"Even if the court ruled differently?" Stix asked.

"To a point," he said. "If the court imposed the death penalty, the warden could inflict it. The court sometimes never said how the prisoner was to die. An' even if they did, it didn't mean that was the way it was gonna happen."

"So what might the warden choose? If someone pissed him off?" I asked.

"At the back of the prison there was a courtyard." He pulled a plan of the prison from a file on his desk and pointed to a small, enclosed area. "There were metal rings in the floor of the courtyard. The prisoner was taken out, usually early in the morning, and laid, face up, on the courtyard floor. The prisoner knew what was coming, so the jailers often had a fight on their hands. They'd shackle the prisoner's hands and feet to the four rings." He spread his hand to illustrate the position of the body. "Then, the guards would remove the door from the prisoner's cell. You've got to remember those doors were hand-carved oak with metal hardware. Bloody heavy, they were. It took three or four guards just to carry one. They'd bring it out into the courtyard and lay it right on top of the prisoner."

It was exactly as Mesmer had described.

I tried not to imagine the crushing weight of the cell door on my body.

"They made a game of it, tried to see how long the prisoner could last. Every day, the guards would stack a new rock on top of the door. The rocks weighed thirty, forty, maybe fifty pounds apiece. The women, they died fairly quickly, maybe three, four days. The guards gave them water and gruel to keep them alive. The record was twelve days."

"Jesus." Stix shook his head.

"Tell me about the triangles," I said and Varney looked at me oddly.

"How'd you know about them, then?" he asked.

"I read it."

"I don't like secrets," he said.

"I'm not keeping any. And a promise is a promise," I reminded him. "I keep my promises."

He thought about what I said before continuing.

"Right. The triangles." Laying the door on you weren't the worst of it," he said. "If the guards didn't like the prisoner, they would lay strips of wood under his back. Or hers. They usually did it to women anyway. Out of spite. The wood was shaped like a triangle. Hang on, I've got one here someplace."

He swivelled around the desk and dug through a pile of stuff on the floor, then passed a triangular-shaped length of dark wood to me. It was nearly three feet long and two and a half inches on each side. The three edges were hard and sharp.

"They'd put one or two of these down under your back. It would cut into you, making the punishment even more unbearable." He took the wooden triangle and rested it behind him. "Especially when they added a new rock. Sometimes, when family or friends visited, they would pay the guards to look the other way. Then they'd climb on the door, maybe four or five people, hoping to kill 'em off quicker. Even then, it took a while to finish them off. Often, all they'd manage to do was bust a few ribs. They'd get off then. They couldn't take the screamin'. So then the poor bastards would have to cope with broken ribs as well."

We sat and looked at Ronald Varney in silence. I wondered what sort of person enjoyed collecting this horror.

"Well," Stix said. "Easy to see why someone would have an aversion to doors."

I would have kicked him but, by then, my kicking foot was really throbbing.

I paid Ronald twenty pounds for a copy of his file.

"I don't suppose —" I tried to make it casual "— anyone else has been asking you about Simmons?"

"Simmons?" He looked thoughtful for a moment. "No. I get lots of people asking about different prisoners. They spend lots of money digging up their family tree. When they find out their great uncle got his neck stretched for murder, they spend twice as much trying to bury it all again."

"But nobody asking specifically about Simmons?"

"None that I can remember, no. And I've got a good memory for stuff like that."

"One last thing," I said. "Have you ever come across a reference to someone called Mesmer working at Newgate Prison?"

"Mesmer?"

"Yes."

"Mesmer who?"

"Dr. Franz-Anton Mesmer. He was around during the early eighteen hundreds."

"Oh, that bloke." He shook his head. "No. There's no mention of him at all. Is he in your manuscript, then?"

"Yes. Don't worry, when this thing is all over, I'll send you a copy. It'll make a very worthy addition to your collection," I told him.

"Can't wait." He rubbed his hands together.

"You're a sick puppy, Mr. Varney," Stix told him.

We stood up to leave.

"I'm an 'istorian," Varney said, indignant now.

"No, you're not." Stix wouldn't leave it alone. "You're a sick little fucker."

I pushed Stix out the door.

"Which," he called out, "is why we like you."

Chapter Twenty-Seven

"WHERE NOW?" Stix asked as we pulled away from Ronald Varney's house.

"Home," I said with a yawn. "I'm ready to call it a night."

"What about the Fiat?"

"I'll call Hertz tomorrow. They can pick it up. Unless the mice get to it first." I took the Fiat keys from him. "I'll get the Mercedes back," I said. "I'll call you in the morning."

I settled down to grab some shut-eye but Stix didn't drive me straight home. He pulled into the emergency parking at Luton Hospital and switched off the engine.

"Where are we?"

"I don't know what you call 'em in Canada," he said "but here we call 'em 'ospitals."

"Aw, come on, Stix. I don't need to go in there."

"Yeah, right. You're bleedin' on my bleedin' upholstery, pal."

I checked the rear-view mirror. The Band-Aids had parted company and my eyebrow was leaking again.

"Oh, son of a bitch."

They kept me waiting almost an hour, by which time I was bleeding steadily. They took me into an overly bright room where a woman doctor in her fifties introduced herself as Dr. McKenzie. She took her time and restitched my eyebrow while I groaned every time she stuck the needle through my aching flesh. When she finished, she showed me the results in a hand mirror. The stitches were much closer together, maybe twice as many as before, and the result was much neater than it had been.

"I'd like to leave it open," she said. "Let the air get to it."

"Okay by me."

"Before he left, your friend said something about your foot?"

Some friend.

"I stepped on something," I said, "in someone's bathroom. But it's fine."

"Show me."

"Really. I've had my fill of needles."

"Maybe you don't need a needle."

I removed my shoe and sock and lay down while the good Dr. McKenzie examined the soul of my foot. It was extremely sore. She came and stood next to me.

"I'd like to freeze it," she said "but inflamed flesh doesn't freeze."

"That's that then."

I started to sit up.

"But there's something in your foot that needs to come out." She pushed me down. "So lie still and go to your happy place."

"My happy place is anywhere but here."

She dug around while I took long, deep breaths and thought of lying next to Cindy Palmer.

"Nearly there," Dr. McKenzie said. "Will you please hold still?"

"I'm ticklish," I answered.

I felt an odd sensation as she removed something from my foot.

"It's a piece of glass," she said.

She came around and showed it to me. It was a wafer-thin piece of curved glass with a tiny blue dot at one end and part of a narrow red line at the other.

"Are you a migrainer?" she asked.

"No. Why?"

"I'm pretty sure that's glass from a phial of DiHydro-Ergotamine."

"Easy for you to say. What's DiHydroglobermine?"

"It's DHE. We use it to help with migraines. We give it intramuscularly."

She turned as if to throw it away but I stopped her.

"Can I have it?"

"If you want."

She put it inside a small plastic bag.

"Is it just for hospital use?"

"Usually."

"Only I stepped on it in a private home. Would a migraine patient have access to it?"

She shrugged.

"It's possible. They would need to inject it themselves. Usually in the thigh. I guess they could get a prescription from their family doctor. We don't use it very often. You need to catch the migraine early for it to really be effective. By the time they come to Emerg, they're usually too far gone for DHE to be of much use."

"You're sure that's what it is?"

"Not one hundred percent."

I didn't say anything.

"I'm guessing it's important," she said.

"It could be."

She nodded, made a decision and patted my thigh.

"Wait here."

She came back holding a tiny, sealed bottle of clear liquid. It looked like an inch-high bowling pin. I held it between my finger and thumb and compared it to the broken piece from the plastic bag.

The bottle had two coloured bands around the narrow part of the neck. The top band was green, the lower band red. Below that was a single, dark blue dot.

It was a perfect match.

"Thank you," I told her. "One last favour. Would you mind writing it down for me?"

Dr. McKenzie wrote the long version of DHE on a piece of paper, then dressed the small tear in my foot. I thanked her again, shook hands and limped out to find Stix waiting in the Jaguar.

I told him everything I'd learned from Dr. McKenzie.

"You think it's a clue?" Stix asked.

"Haven't a clue," I answered bravely. "But it's better out than in."

He dropped me off a hundred yards from the crowd of paparazzi at Sylvia's gate. I ducked under a hedgerow and worked my way to Sylvia's house via other people's back yards. Sylvia no longer warranted police protection. I snuck around front and almost got my key in the door before they saw me.

The barrage of flashbulbs lit up the night sky.

I shut the door quickly behind me.

The house was dark. I felt guilty that I hadn't called Sylvia all day. I moved through the kitchen and down the hall. I found her asleep in her bedroom, the drapes drawn, the television on, the sound turned down. I saw a medicine bottle beside the bed, went in, and had a bad moment when she didn't stir. I picked up the bottle.

Valium.

I read the date and the amount and looked inside. There were still lots left. She'd probably only taken a couple to help her sleep. I turned off the television, pulled the covers up over her shoulders and let her sleep.

I went downstairs and dug up Geoffrey Lansdale's home phone number. It rang fourteen times and I was about to hang up when he finally picked up the phone.

"Yes?"

"Geoffrey?" I said.

"What? Yes. Who's this?"

He sounded half-asleep.

"Eddie Dancer."

"Oh. What do you want?"

Now he sounded pissed off.

"Did Mrs. Lansdale suffer from migraines?"

He waited a moment before answering.

"No. She got headaches but not migraines."

"Would she need an injection of anything? If she had a bad headache?"

"Of course not. What's this about?"

"How about you? Do you suffer from migraines?"

"You're giving me one."

"Is that a yes?"

"It's a no. Neither my wife nor I have ever suffered a migraine."

"And nobody visiting suffers them? A recent visitor, perhaps?"

He was alert now.

"Why are you asking? What have you found?"

"A sliver of glass from a migraine medication. Injectable. It was on the floor in your bathroom. I stepped on it. It was stuck in my foot."

"And you think —"

I cut him off.

"I don't think anything. Yet. I'm simply trying to sort some things out."

"You need to hand it over to the police."

"I intend to," I said.

"You think he may have dropped it?"

"Good night, Geoffrey."

He didn't say anything.

I wanted to ask him how he was bearing up but I wasn't sure we had that sort of relationship.

"Edward?"

"Yes?"

"If you catch him . . ."

He let the sentence hang in the air, though the meaning

was clear. "If you catch him, what will you do to him?"

"I'll stop him."

He asked me how. He wanted details but I couldn't provide him any. Certainly not the details he was looking for, anyway.

He was quiet for a moment, then he sighed.

"Good night, Edward."

He hung up.

I stared at the phone.

"Good night, Geoffrey."

I checked the time and deducted eight hours, took a chance she'd be home and dialed Cindy Palmer back home in Calgary. She picked up on the third ring and the reception was radiant.

"How's it going, Eddie?" She sounded so damn good.

"Confusing," I admitted. "Are you coming in or going out?"

"I'm on the way to work," she said. "But I've always got time for you."

As much as I wanted to talk pillow talk, I needed some fast answers.

"Have you ever heard of DHE?" I asked. "DiHydroErgotamine?"

"Yes. It's a vascular constrictor," she said. "It's a migraine medication."

"Yes," I said, impressed.

"It's either a nasal spray or an intramuscular injection. Do you have a migraine?"

"No. But I think the guy I'm looking for gets them."

"What do you need to know?"

"Everything," I said. "About the injectable stuff."

"Hang on."

I waited while she looked up DHE in one of her medical books.

"Okay," she said. "You want to write this down?"

"Sure."

"It's made by Novartis. Comes in a box of five ampoules. Each ampoule contains one millilitre. It's mixed with half a millilitre of saline and given intramuscularly. Usually with an inch-and-a-half needle, so it goes into the muscle. Probably the outer thigh. You're not going to faint, are you?"

"I might."

"Do you need a minute?"

"Would somebody give it to themselves?" I asked, ignoring her.

"Generally, it's administered at the E.R. but I guess patients could use it themselves. Recommended dose is no more than six a week, so I guess it's possible."

The first glimmer of real hope.

"Can you find out if it's available in the U.K.? If a doctor would prescribe it?"

"I guess so. Can I do it from work? I'm a bit late."

"Of course. I'm sorry. You have my cell number over here?"

"Memorized."

"I love you, Cindy Palmer."

"Who is this?"

She hung up first, giggling.

I made myself a cup of tea and watched some bad British television but I couldn't concentrate. I paced. I sat. I paced some more and after an hour and a half of pacing, my cell phone rang again.

"Hello?"

"Got a pen?" she said, brightly.

"Shoot."

"It's available in the U.K. and it can be prescribed by a doctor. But chances are, he would refer his patient to a clinic. Patients would be taught how to inject themselves properly. After that, their doctor would write the refills. There was a big push just over a year ago. Clinical trials. Three thousand six hundred migrainers signed up at various clinics around the country."

"For DHE?"

"Yes. Some might have got a placebo."

"Can you get their names?"

"You're kidding, right?"

I just thought I'd ask.

"What sort of clinics?"

"Well, headache clinics probably. We have one at the Foothills Hospital. The consultants are mainly neurologists."

"You're amazing," I told her.

"When are you coming home?"

"Soon." I hoped I wasn't lying. "I hope. I don't really know, but this will really help."

"You think the man you're after uses DHE?"

"I think he may." I wanted to ask her something else. "Cindy. When we were talking about Dr. Maurice the other day, did I imagine a change in atmospheric pressure?"

She lowered her voice.

"You might have."

"Anything specific or just woman's intuition?"

"How much do you want to know?"

"As much as you want to tell me."

"Well." I could almost hear the gears grinding. "He thinks he's a bit of a lady's man. He hit on me a couple of times when he was here helping you. Nothing I couldn't handle and he was all very charming, but I know he's married. At least, he wears a wedding ring. But he's quietly persistent. Definitely not my type, though."

"Okay," I said. "Thanks."

"You're not mad at me?" she asked.

Cindy Palmer had issues of self-worth. God knows why because she was worth her weight in uncut diamonds.

"Cindy. I'd be mad if he didn't hit on you."

"That's very sweet of you. Now I've really got to go," she said.

"Love you."

"Love you, too. Just be careful, Eddie Dancer."

I hung up.

I was getting a headache.

Chapter Twenty-Eight

IT WAS GETTING TIRING, scrambling through hedgerows in the wet and the dark, but it was the only way to avoid the paparazzi. I'd considered calling Stix with the DHE update but decided to leave it until morning. The sliver of glass was an important piece of evidence and I walked it up through the town, past the old clock tower, past the Town Hall and the library and up the steps of the police station to the reception desk.

There was a different desk sergeant on duty, a much younger one who sported a huge ginger moustache.

"Is Detective Inspector Newcombe here?" I asked.

He looked me over and gave his ginger moustache a twitch before he answered.

"Who wants to know?"

Put a man in uniform and it goes straight to his head.

"I have evidence in the Gina Lansdale case," I said.

He looked at me some more.

"What's your name?"

"I have evidence in the Gina Lansdale case," I said again. "It's very time-sensitive. Is he here?"

"What you got?"

"Not a lot of patience," I said. "And neither does he."

The moustache twitched again.

"Wait here."

He slid off the stool, moved down the long reception counter and chose a phone out of earshot. He watched me while he spoke on the phone. He came back a minute later.

"You can leave it with me," he said.

"No, I can't."

I turned to leave.

"Hey!"

"If Inspector Newcombe's too lazy to get off his ass and come and see me in person, I'll give it to the paparazzi."

"Oh, fuck." He looked worried now. "He's really busy right now," he said. "Can't you just leave it with me?"

"No. I either give it to him in person, or I give it to them. What's it going to be?"

He grabbed the nearest phone and looked like he was going to be sick. He turned his back on me and had a hasty conversation into the phone. When he hung up, he looked pale.

"He'll be down," he said.

"When?"

"He's on his way," he assured me.

Even so, it still took him ten minutes to get to me. He came into the open reception area at a fast walk and stopped just inches from me. I was used to him by now. He liked to intimidate people by invading their personal space. I leaned towards him until my mouth was almost touching his cheek.

"I still won't sleep with you, Gerry," I said loudly in his ear.

He stiffened and glanced quickly at the reception desk. The ginger moustache suddenly found things to do and Newcombe jerked his head sideways.

"Get over here."

I followed him into an empty office. Neither of us sat down. I placed the baggie on the desk.

"What's that?"

"It's a plastic bag."

He was getting impatient.

"But it's what's in it that counts," I said.

He glanced down, shrugged. He gave up too easy.

"There." I pointed to the sliver of glass in the corner.

He almost put his nose on it.

"What is it?"

"It's a piece of glass," I said. "It came out of my foot. I stepped on it in Mrs. Lansdale's bathroom." I told him all about DHE and that neither Geoffrey nor Gina Lansdale suffered from migraines. I told him about the clinical trials and suggested the real killer might have given himself a shot of DHE while he was in the Lansdales' bathroom.

He looked at me as you would someone you really disliked.

"That's it?" he said, unimpressed.

"That's it," I replied.

"You can leave now," he said.

"I will," I said. "As soon as you write me out a receipt."

He really didn't have a lot of patience. The muscles in

his cheeks flexed rapidly as he clenched his back teeth, biting off his response. Finally, he pulled a notepad from his coat pocket and wrote me a receipt for the sliver of glass. I asked him to date it and he checked his watch, scribbled the date and signed it so hard, he stabbed a hole through the paper when he finished with a period. He tore the receipt from his pad and handed it to me.

I read it, folded it and put it away.

"You're welcome," I told him.

I left him quietly fuming in the empty room. I stepped outside. Somewhere, close by, a bed with my name on it was calling me. The trip to Sylvia's house was a simple reversal. I wriggled through the same wet hedgerows and stumbled through the same ground-floor window into the house. After kicking off my shoes and hanging up my coat, I tiptoed upstairs to check on Sylvia. She hadn't moved. Her breathing was incredibly deep and slow. I moved the bottle of Valium into her bathroom and pulled the bedroom door closed behind me. It was past midnight and I was now feeling the effects of jet lag coupled with bad food. By twelve-thirty, I was under the covers and almost asleep when my cell phone rang again.

It was Cindy.

"Did I wake you?"

"No. Yes. Who cares?"

"I'm sorry. I'm on a break," she said. "Just wanted to hear your voice again."

"Me, too."

We talked longer than her break allowed. We'd been dating almost five months and had never had a real argument, never even raised our voices. She was hard to get to know but I was enjoying the learning. Neither of us wanted to hang up. I heard them paging her.

"Gotta go, Eddie," she said. "We're replacing an eye socket this morning."

So nonchalant.

Like replacing a light bulb.

We hung up together.

Chapter Twenty-Nine

THERE WAS A PICTURE of my bum on page one of Britain's leading tabloid. Some joker had left a copy on the front doorstep, wrapped in plastic to keep the rain off. All in all, not my best side but I was right about the headline.

DOESN'T KNOW HIS ARSE FROM HIS ELBOW

In an insert box, there was a headshot of me resembling a fugitive. It was a copy of the photograph from my Canadian driving licence. Someone had gone to great lengths to get it. Never underestimate the power of the press.

I looked out the kitchen window, pleased that the rain had stopped and what looked like the sun was poking through. Perfect. A dry windshield would really help with my plans. I made coffee, toast, took a shower, changed the band-aid Dr. McKenzie had stuck to the underside of my foot and dressed for another cool day. Sylvia was still asleep and I left her a note. I called Hertz but their office was still closed.

I added a footnote to Sylvia, telling her I'd borrowed her car but if she needed transport, to phone Hertz. I was pretty sure they would bring the Mercedes around to the house.

The paparazzi were another matter. I went looking for something to slow them down and found what I was looking for in a cupboard under the stairs. I found an empty envelope in a kitchen drawer and placed one hundred pounds in twenties inside it, which was part of the cash I now carried since stopping at a bank yesterday. I figured that would cover the cost of the damage I was about to wreak.

I sealed the envelope, put it in my inside jacket pocket and walked boldly out the front door and caught the paparazzi napping.

"Hang about, Eddie!"

Hanging about wasn't an option. I hotfooted it past them, ignoring the cameras and the shouts for a quote. When one of them, walking backwards in front of me, tripped and fell on his butt, I offered him a hand up. But no quotes. Not even a "no comment." I just went about my business, ignoring them. They scrambled to their cars and followed me as I maneuvered Sylvia's black Ford out onto the street. I had a lot to do and didn't want them following me. They were becoming a liability.

The multi-level parking lot was located just off the main street. I drove up the entrance ramp, took a ticket, and the procession of cars followed me to the top floor. We drove across the open parking lot and started down the spiral exit ramp. At the foot of the ramp, I gave the man in the booth my ticket, paid the minimum fee, one pound, waited while he raised the bar to let me out, then handed him the plain white envelope.

"Give this to the man in the car behind me," I said. "Tell him it's to cover the damage."

He looked at the car behind me.

"What damage?" he asked.

I pulled forward just far enough so he could lower the barrier. I watched in the mirror as the procession of cars and SUVs behind me rolled forward, bumper-to-bumper, anxious to stay on my tail.

Then I climbed from the car, shaking my right hand rather vigorously, which might have looked vulgar had it not been for the fact that I was holding something in it.

"This damage," I told the man in the booth.

The paparazzi driver directly behind me realized what was in my hand.

"Ah, fuck!"

He tried to open his door but he was parked too close to the booth and it would only open a few inches. He squirmed in his seat, desperate to get away from me, but he was stuck. He couldn't go forward, he couldn't back up.

I flipped the lid off the aerosol can and sprayed a nice coat of matt black paint evenly across his windshield. Instinctively, he hit the wiper button. The wipers smeared the paint all across his windshield, blinding him completely.

I'd immobilized him in less than five seconds along with the rest of the column.

"You fucker!" He shook his fist out the driver's window. "You'll pay for that!"

"I already have," I said. "You have a nice day."

I placed the paint can on his hood like an ornament. As I drove away, a howling cacophony of horns started up behind me.

When I called Stix and told him of my plans, he agreed to meet me at a gas station in Hendon, close to Derick B. Thomas's flat. I was fairly sure I could find my way there.

The traffic was something else. I tried to keep up but London drivers are very fast. They dart into the tiniest of spaces, squeezing into gaps that seem impossibly small to begin with, and then dart out to gain a car length on the next guy. But I learned quickly and began to enjoy the ride, darting and weaving with the best of them, but even so, I reached Hendon a full half hour later than expected. I followed Stix to the world's most expensive parking lot where I left Sylvia's car for the day and rode south with Stix. We were going back to Crawley. I brought him up to speed on what I'd learned about DiHydroErgotamine.

"Probably won't help much," he said. "Even Newcombe'll have a hell of a time getting information out of the medical profession. It'll take a bleedin' Act of Parliament."

"Assuming he'll take it seriously," I added.

"Yeah. There's that, too."

Which is why we were pursuing Plan B.

I'd phoned Eric Glossard several times already that morning but he was either out or not answering the phone. It was mid-morning by the time we reached Crawley.

Teatime.

We pulled off the main road and found a restaurant still serving breakfast. Stix ordered a bacon sandwich and a pot of tea.

Not just a cup.

An entire pot.

I poured a cup and watched him polish off the rest. His bacon sandwich was two doorstops of white bread dripping hot fat and melted butter that ran down his chin as he chewed his way through it. I could hear his arteries closing with a bang.

"When you're done," I said, "we'll go see if Eric's home, then canvass the High Street."

He wiped his chin clean.

"Right, boss," he said.

I paid for brunch.

It's what good bosses do.

Eric Glossard wasn't home. I banged on his bright yellow door loud enough to wake his neighbours but he still wasn't home. The next-door neighbour, a pasty-faced woman in hair curlers and carpet slippers, came out and told me to "keep the bloody noise down" and that Eric had gone to stay with his sister down in Dorset.

I apologized for disturbing her and we drove to the High Street. Stix parked on a meter and we walked up the side street to Office Copy and Supply, where the long-legged Leah worked.

"Hello again." Leah smiled as I approached the counter.

The air filled with the aroma of coconuts and sunscreen.

"Good morning, Leah," I said. She looked pleased that I'd remembered her name. "You printed off a copy of a manuscript for me yesterday," I said.

"Yes." She nodded, looking concerned. "Did I do something wrong?"

"No, it was fine. But do you remember anyone else coming in for a copy?"

"Of that manuscript?"

"Yes. Maybe two weeks ago?"

"I'm really not sure." She tried hard to think back. "Most people do it themselves."

"So you wouldn't know if some else had made a copy?"

"Not really." She looked disappointed.

"You work here alone?"

"Just me and my dad. Would you like to talk with him?"

"I would," I said and she asked me to wait a moment.

She came back a few seconds later.

"He's on the phone," she said. "But he'll just be a minute." She looked at Stix. "Are you together?"

"Yes," I said. "He's my chauffeur."

"You could always walk back," my chauffeur responded.

Moments later, Leah's father stuck his head around the doorpost.

"You need me, hon?"

He had the same singsong voice as his daughter. Nut-brown eyes, long braided hair topped with a multicoloured woollen cap. I could almost smell the ganja.

"This man wants to ask you about a manuscript, Dad."

Her father came behind the counter looking businesslike but protective of his daughter.

"How can I help you?" he said.

She may have had his voice, but Leah didn't get her long legs from Daddy. He was shorter than she and heavy round the middle.

"I'm looking for someone who might have made a copy of a manuscript." I held up the green binder. "Like this one. Maybe two weeks ago."

I gave him the binder. He flicked through it, frowning.

"Doesn't look familiar," he said, shaking his head, then caught himself and stared at me. "Hey man, I know you. Your picture's in the paper."

"So you don't remember helping anyone copy that?" I ploughed on.

"Is this to do with them murders, man?"

"Did you —" I gave him a hard look "— or didn't you make a copy of that in the last two weeks?"

He handed it back.

"No. I'd remember. What language is that anyway?"

"Italian," I told him. "You're sure?"

"I'm positive. Has this got anything to do with that man who murdered all those women?"

"Maybe." I glanced at Leah. "Is there anywhere else in town that makes copies?"

Leah looked at her dad. They shrugged.

"There was," Leah said. "Dillon's. But they went out of business three or four months ago."

"So there's nowhere else?"

"No." She shook her head. "Unless they did it privately. At somebody's office."

I was afraid of that.

"One last thing." I took out Stix's daughter's sketch of the man who attacked me. "Has this man ever been in the store?"

They studied Sprog's unofficial sketch of Britain's number one serial killer.

"I don't think so." Leah shook her head. "It's so hard to tell from that, though."

"That's not him, is it?" her dad asked. "Is that the bastard they've arrested?"

"Dad!"

"Well, he is a bastard!"

"No." I shook my head. "This is not the man the police arrested."

I took the sketch back.

Another dead end.

"Here." I wrote my name and cell number on the back of one of their business cards. "If you should remember anything, give me a call," I said. "Or if someone who looks like this comes in, you'll call me?"

"Be hard to tell," Leah said.

"Well, he's very tall." I held my hand six inches above my head. "And weighs around three-hundred-and-fifty pounds."

"That's about twenty-two stone," Stix said.

I saw Leah frown. Just a sudden, quick knit of the eyebrows, so subtle, I doubt she even realized she'd done it.

"Leah?" She looked at me quizzically. "You think you might have seen him?"

"Well," she said, then hesitated, unsure. "Not as a customer," she said. "He sounds like a service rep."

I moved to the counter and laid out the sketch again.

"I only got a split-second look." I apologized for the lack of detail. "He was wearing a crash helmet when I saw him."

She paled.

"You know him?"

"The rep who serviced the photocopier rode a motorbike."

"You're sure?"

"Yes. He came in all in leather, carrying a crash helmet."

"What's his name?"

She shook her head.

"I don't know," she said. "He's only been here that one time."

"When?"

"Last time it was serviced. A few weeks ago."

"Who services your copiers?"

"Service Master, in North London. We usually call them. He said he was in the area, just stopped by to give it a tune-up. A freebie," Leah said. "Oh, God. Dad."

Leah's father wrapped his arm around her shoulder.

"S'all right, luv."

"Do you keep a service record?" I asked him.

"Under the copier. In the service logbook."

He left Leah and moved to the Canon copier on the shop floor. The logbook sat in a small slot beneath the machine. He pulled it out, flipped to the last page, pointed to an entry.

"Here," he said, handing me the book. "I can't read it without my glasses."

But I could.

It was a one-line entry.

The date.

And a signature.

I stared in disbelief.

It was dated the same day Maria Glossard was murdered.

And it was signed: *Thomas Simmons.*

Chapter Thirty

THE LOGBOOK SHOWED Service Master's address as Cricklewood, North London. I wrote down their street address and phone number. It was Saturday but I called them anyway. After four rings, I got a recording telling me they were open Monday to Friday from eight-thirty to five, closed weekends and holidays. There was no provision to leave a message.

We were in the car, heading back to London.

"He obviously copied the manuscript," I told Stix as he threaded his way rapidly through the northbound traffic.

"Or maybe he's just fuckin' with your 'ead," he said.

"It was almost two weeks ago, Stix. He'd never heard of me two weeks ago."

"So how'd he get hold of the manuscript?"

"Maria must have been in the store when he was servicing the copier. Maybe he made the copies for her. The point is, we can place him there the day Maria was murdered. That's good enough for me."

"Maybe its just coincidence," he said.

"I don't believe in coincidence."

"I still think Mesmer got it right," he said. "I think this guy's been around the block a few times already."

"I know what you believe," I said. "You believe in reincarnation. You believe in rebirth and the whole re-embodiment thing. But I don't, Stix. I think we get one go-around and when it's over, it's over. Doesn't mean you don't try to live your life the best you can. Just means the train only stops here once."

"How do you explain the similarities, then?"

"There are no similarities," I said. "They're just self-fulfilling prophesies. He read the translation, decided to act out Mesmer's reincarnated tales of murder and mayhem. He's a wacko, what more can I tell you? I don't know what he is, but I know what he isn't. He isn't some reincarnated spirit from the eighteen hundreds coming back for a second helping."

"You had your fingers crossed when you said that."

"Bullshit."

He shot through an impossibly narrow gap between a pair of double-decker buses and turned sharp left down a long narrow side street. We both fell quiet after that. He knew London better than a cabbie and didn't need the A to Z to find Service Master's office. It was in a business park of two-storey glass and metal buildings, each set back from the service road that looped through the park. Each building had a small, grassy area out front with staff parking around the back. Service Master occupied an entire building, a tall, single-storey, grey-brick and glass structure, maybe eight thousand square feet. We drove carefully around the block. Saturday was a quiet day for business.

"What's the plan?" Stix wondered.

"Most of the time," I admitted, "I don't have one. I just blunder around until something occurs to me. Or someone shoots me."

"That's a good plan. Makes me feel real safe. Anything occurring?"

"Drive round the back."

There was a loading bay with a pair of steel shutter doors and, to the far left, a windowless steel door. A sticker on the door warned of an alarm. I ran my fingers over the door. If it was alarmed, and I had no doubt it was, we could get through it but we would have to be patient.

"Do you have a tire iron?" I asked Stix.

He went to the trunk and came back with a two-foot-long metal brace that operated the Jag's car jack.

"This do?"

"Let's find out."

I wedged the brace in the top corner of the door, opposite the hinges, and pried it open a quarter inch. Instantly, I heard an alarm shriek from inside the building. I handed the brace back to Stix.

"Let's take a drive," I said.

It took them eight minutes. Two blue security cars with light bars on the roof. Wannabe cops. And one car of the real thing. We watched from a hundred yards away while they entered the building via the back door. The cops went in first. After less than ten minutes, the cops came out. One of the security guys must have said something funny because everyone laughed. The cops left first, then the security guys left together. I gave them a five-minute head start before I tripped the alarm again.

The two security cars were back in less than ten minutes but no cops this time. The four guards went through the place thoroughly, shrugged at one another and drove away again. I gave them twelve minutes, then tripped it again. They took fifteen minutes, and while they were there, a dark blue BMW pulled around back.

The owner.

He went inside and we watched for another twenty minutes before they all came out. The owner pulled out a cell phone and made a call. He shook hands with two of the four security guards and they followed him out of the parking lot.

I tripped it again three minutes later but the alarm was silent. I wrenched hard on the door but the alarm was mute.

"They turned it off," I said. "Give me a minute."

Stix stood back and watched me as I went to work on the door lock. If they'd strip-searched my on-board luggage at the airport really, really thoroughly, I'd be serving a three-to-five stretch for carrying a set of picks and hooks. But they were packed away so well, they avoided X-ray detection and I remained a free man. The thin metal picks were nestled inside a fat, silver-coloured pen that contained enough ink I could write a short confession, should anybody ever figure it out.

Picking the door lock took a minute and a half.

"We're in." I opened the door. "But you don't have to come."

"You're sure the alarm's off?" he asked.

"No."

"You're sure there's no guard dogs?"

"No."

"You're sure there's no machine-gun posts?"

"No."

"Sounds like fun. Let's go."

He pushed in ahead of me and I followed him down a long corridor to the front office. There was an open area with a receptionist's desk and two sets of filing cabinets. We began a systematic search. I flipped through the Rolodex, the telephone message pad, the filing cabinets, all without success. There was no Thomas Simmons on file in the system. I'd hoped to find an employee list, with their names and addresses spelled out neatly in alphabetical order. There wasn't one. But I did find a payroll ledger that had everyone's name and employee number on it.

No addresses or phone numbers, though.

And no Thomas Simmons anywhere.

We moved through the individual offices. Three were locked but I had them all open within a couple of minutes. They gave up nothing. At the far end, there was a staff lunchroom with a well-equipped kitchen and a large fridge. We backtracked and came to the service area at the rear of the building. It was a large, open room, almost half the entire office area. Dozens of photocopiers stood around in various states of repair while dozens of smaller machines sat on a long workbench running almost the entire length of the building. A shelf ran below the entire bench, cluttered with copier parts. We searched methodically, opening drawers, reading personal stuff. We became separated, working fifty, sixty feet apart.

After fifteen minutes, I was about to call it a day when Stix suddenly froze.

"What?" I whispered but then I heard it myself.

Someone was in the building with us.

There were two voices.

Two men, talking back and forth. I climbed onto the shelf under the workbench and Stix followed suit.

But only just in time.

It was two of the original security guards, coming back to check the building. I was glad we left the Jaguar parked on the far side of the street.

If they thought anyone was in the building, they weren't acting like it. It was just a routine check. Or at least it was until they found the unlocked office doors.

My bad.

I heard a radio crackle as one of the guards called for backup. I wriggled deeper beneath the workbench. The wide shelf was cluttered with copier stuff, rollers, lids, trays and electronic components. I gingerly moved a few parts and slid down behind them. I could hear Stix farther up the room.

"You noisy sod," I whispered to him.

"Hey, Eddie!" he whispered back. "What if they've got a dog?"

I hadn't thought of that.

"Thanks," I whispered. "For nothing."

I reached down and turned off my cell phone. Didn't need that going off at an inopportune moment. We lay behind a small mountain of gear, breathing quietly while the guards worked their way through the building. Within minutes, they were joined by two more.

It was getting hot. I needed to scratch myself in half a dozen places. I heard someone come into the work area, heard him walk the length of the room. A second guard joined him.

"Anything?"

"Fuck all," the guard farthest from me replied. "I bet twat face left them fucking doors unlocked."

"You think?"

"Sure. Ain't nobody here, is there?"

"Doubt it."

"Wasting our time then, aren't we."

"We tried calling him. All we got was his answer machine."

"Try his mobile."

"I will."

I heard him key his radio mike.

"It's Walter. D'you have Ackerman's mobile number?"

A female voice fired a number back

"Ta, love."

He shut the two-way mike off and switched to his mobile phone. I heard the musical beeps as he tapped Ackerman's mobile phone number into his keypad.

There was silence for maybe twenty seconds before the guard spoke. He'd leaned against the workbench. He was less than five feet from me.

"This is Walter Phillips of Pro Security, Mr. Ackerman. We are doing a routine walk-through of your premises again and found three unlocked doors on the inside. Can you call me on my direct line? It's four-two-seven. Three-triple-eight. I'll wait for your call."

He snapped the phone shut.

"Hey, Walt!" It was the guard at the other end of the long room. "Do we all have to stay here until dickweed calls back?"

"That's the rule," Walter told him.

"Jesus Christ, Walt!"

"I don't make the rules, Paul."

Paul muttered something I couldn't hear, and a door banged shut.

So. Mr. Ackerman was going to phone back to instruct the guards to lock down the building, call up reinforcements and search the place top to bottom.

Sooner or later, they were going to find us.

I heard Walter talking on the radio again but he was moving away and I couldn't catch what he said. Then I heard the door bang shut. I guessed Walt had gone to the main office.

I considered our options. We could stay put and hope for the best.

The Ostrich Option.

Or we could roll out from under the workbench, kill the guards and go and have a cup of tea.

The Really Extreme Option.

Or we could pray.

The Religious Option.

A whispered "Shit!"

"Oh, ye of little faith," I whispered back.

"Oh, fuck faith," he whispered at me. "Walter-By-the-Book just called for police backup."

So that's what he was doing.

Plan D it was, then.

The Ackerman Option.

I worked my cell phone out of my pocket, turned it on and dialed up Walter's direct number.

The one I'd memorized.

Four-two-seven. Three-triple-eight.

I just hoped neither of the guards decided to return to the service area.

I held the phone hard to my ear. I could hear it ringing out in the corridor. It rang three times before Walter answered it.

"Phillips," Walter answered.

"It's Ackerman, Mr. Phillips," I put on my best British whisper. "I got your message. My fault. I forgot to lock those doors behind me."

His pause was full of suspicion.

"Are you all right, sir?"

"Of course."

"You seem to be whispering."

"I'm in a public library. They frown on people yelling on a cell phone."

"Right, sir. Shall we lock them up behind us?"

"Please," I said. "Sorry for the trouble, Walter."

"No trouble at all, sir," he said. I heard him very clearly, because he'd just stepped into the service room. "Thank you for calling back so promptly."

I could see his shoes. I didn't dare breathe.

"Sir?" He stood waiting. "Mr. Ackerman? Hello?"

Oh, crap.

I waited. He didn't move. The line was still open. I was amazed he couldn't hear his own voice coming over my cell phone. Just when I was ready to explode, he stepped back into the corridor.

". . . my appreciation at Christmas, Walter," I said.

"Beg pardon, sir?"

"I think we got a bad connection for a moment," I said. "I was just saying I hope you'll let me show my appreciation at Christmas, Walter."

"Well, thank you very much, sir."

"I have to go," I whispered. "It's public flogging day at the library."

"Of course. Thank you, Mr. Ackerman."

I closed the cell phone and let out a long breath.

"Public flogging day?" hissed Stix.

"You don't have that in England?" I said. "Never mind. Let's get the hell outa here."

But things, of course, are never that easy.

A ways off, down the outside corridor, I heard a phone ringing. It had the same ring tone as Walter Phillips's mobile phone. I slid from beneath the workbench, tiptoed to the door, held it open an inch and heard Walt answer his phone.

"Phillips." There was a brief pause. "Mr. Ackerman?"

Crap!

Double crap!

Stix was half in, half out of the storage shelf. I tugged him loose and shoved him towards the loading bay doors.

"May I make a suggestion?" I asked.

He was brushing dust from his pant legs.

"What?"

"Run."

We ran to the bay doors.

The doors were metal roll-ups with an electric motor and chains at the side for manual override. I could hear Walter Phillips yelling for backup. I pressed the green UP button. The door began moving then stopped suddenly, the motor humming in protest.

Stix grabbed a handful of chain but the door was jammed.

I looked along the side rail. There was a locking device with a thin red handle. I wrenched the handle.

A metal-on-metal screech and the roll-up door closed.

And stayed closed.

I hit the green button again and the door began its long and arduous climb upwards.

There was a six-inch gap at the bottom of the door when Walter Phillips and the other three guards burst into the room.

"Stop!" one of them yelled.

Then the clatter of leather shoes on concrete as they came racing towards us.

Nine inches.

Oh, crapola!

Stix threw himself face down, rolled under the door and disappeared. I followed suit, tearing the back of my shirt in the process. There was a short stretch of dock with a five-foot drop to the parking lot. Stix was already down, scrambling to get his legs under him. I jumped, landed hard and took off after him. We sprinted fast towards open ground while behind us, Walt Phillips was yelling, telling the other three guards to head us off.

For a skinny guy with four pounds of metal on his head, Stix could run. I loped along beside him and we rounded the corner of the building like a pair of runaways. It seemed foolish to head for the Jag but we did it anyway. We sprinted hard across the public parking lot, across the lawn, and over the ornamental shrubbery in a single bound. We sprinted down the sidewalk and onto the road. Stix pointed his automatic car door opener at the Jag, and I saw the passenger door lock jump open.

I was inside a split second after him. As he fumbled with the ignition key, two of the guards rounded the corner of the building.

Not close enough to read his licence plate.

I hoped.

I heard the engine crank over, felt it catch, then shot forward into the dash when Stix threw it into reverse and backed away from the guards at high speed. The gearbox protested loudly at the impossible burst of speed and the car rocked on its springs. Stix held it steady, spun the wheel hard right and slammed on the emergency brake. The rear wheels locked up and the car spun through a rubber-burning one-eighty. He took it out of reverse, let off the brake, slammed it into first and stomped the gas. The Jag fishtailed the first fifty yards before the tires bit into the asphalt and we were away. He checked the rear-view mirror, settled the car down and ripped into a sharp right-hander that would have flipped a lesser car on its roof.

When we reached the main road, the traffic was heavy,

slowing us down. He cursed and drove straight across. He might have had his eyes closed and his fingers crossed as he did so. I looked back and saw the two security cars behind us. We turned into a residential neighbourhood full of kids and kept our speed down. We were maybe a hundred and fifty yards ahead when the first security car turned in behind us.

Stix cursed again and made a hard left.

Another residential street. Cars parked on the street and in the driveways. And, on our left, a house with an attached garage. The garage door was open, the garage empty. Stix didn't hesitate. He wheeled the Jag hard left and gunned it up the drive. He pulled into the garage, out of sight, and we slid down the seats like kids in trouble. He adjusted the mirror and we leaned in, knocking heads as we watched both security cars shoot past the driveway, oblivious to us.

"Faked 'em out." He grinned.

We sat there for a few seconds, getting our breath back.

And there was a sharp tap on the driver's side window.

A man stood next to the car. Stix powered down his window, and an irate homeowner glared at the pair of us.

"So," Stix said. "Is Jerry ready?"

"What?"

"Jerry? Is he ready?"

"What the hell are you talking about?" the man said.

"Is this number seventeen?"

"It's not even close. Now get the hell out of my garage."

"Oh." Stix smiled politely. "Sorry, mate. My mistake."

We reversed down the drive. There was no sign of the security cars and we drove quickly to the main road where we finally lost ourselves in London's heavy traffic.

"And I thought being a paparazzi was dangerous," Stix said, finally. "You do that stuff often?"

"All the time."

We drove in silence for a while after that.

Then my bladder began to ache.

That's the thing about tea.

You only ever rent it.

Chapter Thirty-One

WE STOPPED FOR A bathroom break, then more tea and cookies. My stitches seemed overly tight and my head was pounding from running. We had performed an illegal act that could have gotten us locked up but we'd found nothing on Thomas Simmons. Not that I believed that was his real name. It just proved, beyond a doubt, he had read Mesmer's manuscript.

He'd been in the store when Maria made her copy of the manuscript. He'd read the damned thing. Anything else was just hocus-pocus.

"So what's the new plan, boss?" Stix dunked a digestive biscuit in his mug of tea.

"Haven't decided," I said, as though I had a multitude of options and hadn't decided which one to choose.

"That bad, eh?"

He dunked another cookie.

And his cell phone rang.

He swallowed the cookie before answering.

And all the blood drained from his face.

"Jesus Christ, Sharon!"

He was shouting.

People in the café turned and stared in our direction.

"Call them!" He listened a moment longer. "Jesus Christ!"

He hung up and stood rapidly. I threw money on the table to cover the bill as Stix turned and ran out.

"Stix!" I caught up with him. He seemed dazed and I saw the look of horror on his face.

"It's Sprog," he said. "He took Sprog this afternoon. Sharon was on a break, someone came to the front desk, wanted to see one of the rooms. Sprog took him up to show him. She never came back. That was maybe two hours ago."

"How do you know it's him?"

"He phoned Sharon. Said to tell us he's the man of blood murder."

Blood, murder?

That was what it said in Ronald Varney's file about Thomas Simmons.

A man of Blood, Murder.

And something else.

We were in the car, Stix over-revving the motor. He slipped the clutch and we screamed into traffic, incurring a wrath of horns.

"Jesus Christ!" Stix smacked the steering wheel. "He's got Angie! He's got my kid!"

He looked at me, a brief moment, a look that said it was my fault, and I couldn't blame him, couldn't deny it.

"Did she call the police?"

"Yes. Shit!"

We were driving very fast.

"Where are we going?" I tried to sound calm.

"What?"

He barely missed the front of a bus.

"Where are we going?" I tried again.

"Bayswater."

"Why?"

"That's where she was!"

"But she's not there anymore." I tried to slow him down. "And we won't make Bayswater the way you're driving."

"Then where?" he screamed. "Then fuckin' where?"

We drove fast through heavy traffic, cutting back and forth between lanes. He was beyond reason, in a place I couldn't reach.

All I could do was buckle up and pray. As he shot through impossible gaps, almost scraping paint, laying on the horn and flashing his brights, I tried to talk him down. I had no idea where we were headed and I doubt he did, either. He was driving on pure adrenalin, his reflexes jacked, his vision narrowed to a single dot.

"You've got to slow down, Stix!" I was almost shouting. "You'll be no use to her if you're dead!"

He hit the steering wheel hard with his palm, cut in front of a taxi, and I felt the Jag slide in a four-wheel drift across a traffic circle, a major roundabout full of traffic.

And then I saw it out of the corner of my eye.

A green exit sign flashed by.

I don't believe in coincidence.

Or happenstance.

Or quirks of fate.

But maybe, just maybe, I believe in signs.

"Again." I circled with a finger.

"What?"

"Go around again!"

He pulled the wheel away from his intended exit. The tires squealed loudly but he held his line, circling all the way around until we came upon the road sign again.

"There." I pointed at it.

It said Hertford.

"Take that one," I told him.

"Why?"

We missed it.

"Go round again!" I yelled at him. "It's what it said, goddammit! Varney's file. It said 'Man of blood, murder. Hertford.' That's what that sign says! Hertford!"

He looked over but didn't argue, steered the Jag into the Hertford exit as we came around for the third time.

Man of blood, murder. Hertford.

That's what it had said.

I hadn't understood the word *Hertford.*

"It's where he lives," I said.

"How can you know that?" He was practically shouting and was still driving way too fast.

"Slow down, concentrate on the road, the last thing we need is a wreck. Ronald Varney's file said *Blood, Murder, Hertford.* I didn't realize Hertford was a town."

"Oh, Christ." He slowed down. "I remember."

"It's a long shot, but he won't still be in Bayswater, I'm sure of that."

While he drove, I called Directory Enquiries to see if

they had a listing for Thomas Simmons in Hertford.

They did.

Well, almost.

They had a T. Simmons. The operator gave me his phone number. I risked calling, listening while the phone rang on for an eternity without answer. I let it ring twenty times before hanging up. I called Directory Enquires back and asked for the street address.

"We're not allowed to give out that information."

I hung up, cursing.

The next road sign said Hertford, thirty-seven miles. Stix kept one hand on the stick shift and drove the damn car like it was stolen.

We came to the outskirts of Hertford and I waved him over to a gas station with a phone booth. I sent him inside for a street map while I rifled the pages of the phone book. I ripped out SHE to SMID and ran to the car. T. Simmons was listed at 32 Meddings Lane.

I unfolded the street map and gave Stix directions. Meddings Lane was on the north side of town and we'd come in from the south. It took fifteen minutes to find it. Rich neighbourhood, big homes set back from the road, large lots beautifully landscaped.

Number 32 was a big, red-brick home, overgrown with ivy clinging to the brickwork. A paved drive curved from the road. Stix never hesitated. He wheeled the Jag fast up the drive, slammed on the brakes and skidded to a stop that rocked the car sideways. He was out of the car before I could stop him. He pounded on the door, found the bell button, pressed it repeatedly.

It rang hollowly from deep inside.

I unlocked the SIG Sauer from the glovebox and worked my way around the side of the house to the rear garden. The land rose steeply towards a copse of trees. Manicured lawns and stone retaining walls, beds of roses and a small greenhouse set back from the side of the house.

I saw a movement inside and flicked off the safety.

Whoever was inside had no idea I was coming. The door was partially open and I stepped quickly inside. The greenhouse was thirty feet long and maybe twelve feet across. He stood with his back to me, hunched over a potting bench. He was far smaller than my assailant, thinner and much older. He wore a loose-fitting brown cardigan and brown cord trousers. His hair was thin and wispy and hadn't been cut in a while.

I scraped an empty pot across the floor with my foot.

He stopped, straightened, turned to face me.

"Yes?"

He looked slightly annoyed.

"Mr. Simmons?"

"Who are you?"

"Eddie Dancer. Are you Thomas Simmons?"

"No, you damn fool, I'm Terrence Simmons," he said. "What do you want?"

"Do you have a son?"

"I have two daughters."

"That's not what I asked."

"I just told you." He paused, frowned at the gun. "Is that what I think it is?"

"Yes."

"You need a gun to ask questions of an old man?"

"Maybe."

"Who are you?"

"A private detective."

"Are you allowed to carry that?"

"No."

"I didn't think so." He rubbed soil from his fingers. "Ask me what you need to know, then get off my property."

"Do you have a relative named Thomas Simmons?"

"No. I don't."

"I'm sorry to have troubled you," I said and put the gun away.

"And put that pot back. It keeps the door open."

I moved the pot back and left him to his roses.

Stix was trying to find an unlocked window.

"It's not him," I said.

He looked ready to kill.

"How'd you know?"

"Trust me." I steered him back to the car. "He's an old man with two daughters. It's not him, Stix. It's not."

He drove through Hertford in seething silence. I stared out the window, totally at a loss. It was an old town, lots of red-brick buildings, lots of two-storey shops crowding the narrow road. Names flashed by. Hertford Ales. Best Bespoke Tailoring. Advantage Accounting. Twice Is Nice. Dillon's. Ace Hardware. Abbie's Deli and Gift Emporium.

Dillon's?

Chapter Thirty-Two

"STOP THE CAR."

He stared at me.

"Stop!"

He pulled onto the sidewalk, the motor running.

"Wait here."

"Where are you going?"

I didn't answer, just jumped out and ran down the narrow street.

Dillon's Office Supply.

Dillon's was the name of the store in Crawley. The one Leah said had gone out of business because the old man had died.

I tried the door.

It was locked. I peered in. A short counter, shelves of binders, pens, stationery. A photocopier in the far corner. The sign on the door said they were open Monday through Friday, nine to five-thirty. There was no other information, no name, no number to call in an emergency. I went next door. The accounting office was closed.

Further down the block, the tailor was open.

His little bell almost fell off its bracket when I flung the door open. A thin, sad-looking Indian gentleman in a dark three-piece suit stood to attention beside a long cutting table.

"How may I help you, please?" he said.

"Who owns that stationery store?" I said, pointing up the road.

He shook his head. "I do not wish to know them," he said. "They are rude people."

"What's their name?"

"I don't know their name," he said. "They are rude. They call me Paki," he said. "I am clearly Indian."

"Right," I said but he looked unconvinced. "Do you know where they live?" I asked.

"Of course not," he said. "They are rude. Thank you. Have a nice day. Would you like a suit?"

I left the door open as I ran back out.

I went next door to Hertford Ales. It was a room, off a pub, selling liquor. A large, jovial lady came around from the bar.

"Yes, luv?" She gave me a warm smile.

"Do you know who owns Dillon's up the street?" I asked.

"Well, the old man died a while back. I guess his son owns it now."

"Do you know his name?"

"Yeah." She tucked a lock of stray hair into her bun. "Martin. Funny bugger. Not funny har-har," she said and twirled her finger alongside her temple. "More, funny peculiar."

"What does he look like?"

"Can't say's I've ever noticed," she said. "Not my type, though."

"How big is he?"

"Oh, he's a big bugger. Way bigger'n you." She turned. "Hey Bernie, how big's Martin Dillon?"

"Bloody huge," a voice replied.

"Does he," I said, "ride a motorcycle?"

"Does he ride a bike?" she yelled.

"I dunno! What you keep askin' me for?"

"Do you know where he lives?" I pushed on.

"Do you know where he lives?" she yelled.

"Christ, Mary! I'm tryin' to work over here!"

"Hang on," she said to me and disappeared around the bar. A few moments later, a bald man with a green apron stepped around in her place.

"He lives on Ford Street," he said to me without waiting for an introduction. "End house. On the right. Reason I know, he printed our business cards. I had to go up there to pick 'em up 'cause the old man had died. Last week of July. Reason I remember that is 'cause her sister, Elsie, died the week before. That cancer's a bastard though, innit?"

"Thanks." I headed for the door, turned around. "You ever see him on a bike with a sidecar?"

"Oh, that thing. Yeah. He rides it all the time."

"Thanks again," I said.

"Any time," he said. "Watch him, though," he cautioned. "He's a big bastard, that one. A bit of a nutter, to tell you the truth."

"I know." I pulled the door open.

"What happened to your 'ead?" he asked.
"He did." I shut the door behind me.
But now it's my turn.

Chapter Thirty-Three

"WHERE'VE YOU BEEN?" Stix asked, as I climbed in beside him.

"There's a Dillon's here. Same as the one shut down in Crawley. It's run by Martin Dillon. His father died in July. Martin Dillon's six-five and a bit of a nutter."

Stix stared at me.

"And he rides a bike. A combination, bike and sidecar."

"Christ." He was barely breathing, his eyes big as saucers.

"And he lives on Ford Street."

He threw the road map at me as we bounced off the sidewalk back onto the road. I found Ford Street and directed Stix through a maze of streets.

It took us barely eight minutes to get there.

We turned onto Ford Street slowly, taking in every house.

It wasn't a cul-de-sac. The houses on the left continued up the street while the houses on the right ended beside a field of overgrown grass and scraggly trees. It was a rundown street, full of potholes and loose gravel. The homes were even worse. Very neglected, some boarded up, the lawns overgrown, gates hanging off, paint peeling around cracked windows, sheets in place of drapes, dead cars in the front yards.

"Slow." I waved my hand to keep the speed down.

We cruised slowly past Martin Dillon's house. It was on a much larger lot than all the rest, maybe an acre or so, isolating it from the other homes. It also showed signs of decay. Narrow cracks in the brickwork ran halfway up the side of the two-storey home. There were tiles missing from the roof, paintwork flaking from the trim. The house looked vacant, though it was hard to tell because the drapes were all tightly closed.

I checked both sides of the street. There was no sign of a motorcycle and sidecar parked anywhere. We rolled past Dillon's house and parked a block away on the opposite side.

Stix was out of the Jag in a heartbeat. He opened the trunk and retrieved a flat tire iron designed to pop the wheel rims from the Jaguar.

We walked quickly back to the house.

A large detached garage stood behind the house to the left, close to an undernourished patch of trees. There was no access to the garage from the front of the house.

"There's a back lane," I said. "Give me a couple minutes. When I get to the back door of the house, hammer on the front."

The grass was wet and slippery underfoot. I worked my way around to the back of the garage, staying out of sight. The garage was set at an angle, about fifty feet from the back of the house. The side door was locked. The up-and-over door, too.

There were fresh tire tracks in the soft mud.

I counted them.

They were in sets of three.

The windows were painted over. I used a sharp-edged stone and scraped off some paint.

There was no motorcycle in the garage.

I worked my way quickly to the back of the house. The door was locked. I waved Stix to the front door. The quiet was broken when we simultaneously pounded on the doors. I stepped back to watch for curtain movement.

There was none.

It was obvious Martin Dillon was not home. But he had a couple of hours start on us and I was sure that he'd been back during that time, based on the tire tracks.

The old sash windows on the ground floor had been painted over. They hadn't been opened in twenty years. I went around to the front. Stix was rattling the front door handle.

He hammered on the front door again. I stepped back and watched for any telltale flicker of drape.

Still nothing.

The house was empty.

"Goddamn shit!" Stix kicked the front door.

"Cover me."

I unloaded my lock pick set and went to work on the front door lock. It was old and could have used a quart of oil, which is why it took me a full minute to get the damn thing open.

"We're in," I said.

Spoken too soon.

A heavy-duty security chain caught the door. It was barely wide enough to admit a cat.

A real skinny one.

"Dammit."

Stix offered to jimmie the door with the tire iron but the noise would wake the dead.

I shut the door and we moved around back. That door took me less than a minute.

"Okay. Now we're in," I said.

But we weren't.

It was the weirdest thing.

The back door had a security chain locked in place too.

If he wasn't home, how the hell could he lock the front and back doors from the inside?

There was no other way in.

Or out.

I shut the door.

"You think he's in there?" Stix asked.

"If he is, where's his bike?"

"It's not in the garage?"

"Not unless he buried it."

Which was a thought.

There was a covered inspection pit in the middle of the garage floor.

We moved fast.

I scratched a larger peephole in the garage window. We cupped our hands and peered in. It was hard to tell if the inspection pit was wide enough to hide a bike.

There was no time for finesse. I took the tire iron and jimmied the side door. It gave with a sharp crack that disturbed a bunch of crows watching from the skeletoid limbs of a nearby tree. They cawed loudly and circled the garage in protest.

We stepped inside and I hammered the splintered wooden shards of the doorjamb back in place. It would pass a brief inspection.

"It stinks," Stix said.

He was right but I was already on the move. The garage was fairly empty, just a few wall shelves with rusted cans of old paint and some rotting stacks of newspaper. Nowhere to hide a fourteen year old, let alone a motorcycle. The back of the garage held a metal lathe and a study workbench with a drill press and a sizeable vice.

Neither of us wanted to think about what Martin Dillon made on that lathe.

It sure as hell wasn't parts for his motorcycle.

I found the finger ring in the floor and opened the inspection cover all the way. Below me was a three-feet-wide by eight-feet-long inspection pit. No space to hide a motorcycle with a bulky sidecar.

No Angie, either.

But at the far end of the pit, closest to the house, a set of steps led down into the darkness.

"Hold this." I handed the cover to Stix and dropped five feet to the bottom of the narrow pit. It was dark and I made my way to the bottom of the rough-cut steps.

Stix followed me, letting the inspection pit cover fall back in place behind him just as I found the light switch.

Pale electric light filled the pit.

Up ahead, a heavy piece of carpet hung over a makeshift opening.

I rolled the edge of the carpet back.

And wished I hadn't.

Chapter Thirty-Four

"JESUS! WHAT'S THAT SMELL?"

I thought Stix was going to throw up.

"Sewage," I said. "Breathe through your mouth."

"I do that, it feels like I'm eating it." He paused. "You're not going in there?"

"No." I said. "We are."

Ahead of us snaked a man-made tunnel. It was at best four feet wide and maybe five feet high. A string of twenty-five-watt naked light bulbs hung from the undulating ceiling. It looked like something from Auschwitz.

Sections of dirt spilled out where the plywood ceiling had rotted away. Two-by-fours bowed dangerously in the putrid air. Not just raw sewage now.

Something worse.

The smell of things rotting, things buried in the earth for eons. The tunnel, buried ten feet beneath the surface of the earth, connected Martin Dillon's garage to the basement of his house.

We ducked into it.

The lights jiggled eerily, throwing grotesque shadows across the walls as we worked our way carefully up the tunnel. I held the SIG Sauer straight out, finger on the trigger, the safety off. If as much as a mouse had stepped out, I'd have blown it apart. The floor was mud. Soft, wet mud that oozed up over the tops of my shoes. It reeked of decay with every step. The ceiling and walls leaked moisture around us. We bent forward, keeping close to the right-hand wall, away from a running sore of raw sewage that seeped underfoot.

The tunnel measured about fifty feet in length. I tried not to think about the tons of earth compacted above our heads, tried not to think what would happen if the ground shifted, if the tunnel caved in, if Martin Dillon suddenly appeared around a corner.

It was slow going.

And boiling hot.

The air was stagnant. Heavy and unmoving. And we were barely halfway.

Breathe through your mouth, dammit.

The smell became sharper, stronger.

Overpowering now.

Ahead, a thick metal pipe angled across our path, two feet off the ground. It was a wrought iron sewer pipe. There was a flange in the center, joining two sections. Without support, and with Martin Dillon using it as a step, the flange had split, and raw sewage leaked out. Bent double, we stepped over the pipe, trying not to walk in the filthy swill.

I looked down and saw something else.

Something I didn't want to see.

There wasn't only raw sewage coming out of that pipe.

There were thick white bone chips.

Like skull fragments.

I tightened my grip on the SIG Sauer, held my breath another ten feet, exhaled. I could see more heavy carpeting ahead, cut slightly larger than the doorway it concealed.

Thank God.

We were almost at the house.

A moment to wipe my hands, to dry the sweat beading in the palm of my gun hand. I rubbed sweat from the gun and stood before the heavy carpet, listening for signs of life.

Even with Stix breathing in my ear, the silence was deafening.

I took a long, deep breath, then moved the curtain aside an inch.

Then another.

Light from the tunnel fell into a wider passageway ahead of us. I reached in, found a pair of light switches, picked one and the passageway ahead lit up.

I turned the tunnel lights off.

The lit passageway appeared empty.

We stepped through the opening, into the basement of Martin Dillon's house. We were at the far end of a long passageway. Five feet wide and nine feet high. The string of ceiling lights continued along the centre of the new passageway. We counted five doors, three to the left, two to the right. Massive wooden doors that hung from heavy iron hinges set in solid concrete walls.

Ugly doors.

Like doors on the death cells of a Third World jailhouse.

The first cell to our right was missing its door. We barely

breathed as we drew level. Dim light fell across the threshold. The floor was filthy, marked by dark red stains around a circular floor drain. And, set around the drain at intervals, four sets of rusted metal shackles, anchored to the concrete floor.

I signalled Stix I was going in.

He looked pale but didn't argue.

I had the gun.

A quick breath and I backed in, staying low. The gun was a blur as I made a fast sweep of the inside corners. They were empty. I dropped my gun arm, exhaled and stepped back out.

Stix was examining the locks on the cell doors. They were secured with heavy-duty, shotgun-safe padlocks.

If Angie were inside any of them, I wasn't going to be able to pick my way in to save her.

One of the doors had a peephole, set high, but the angle was wrong and we couldn't see anything inside. We called to Angie and listened at every cell.

But if she was in there, she was deathly quiet.

Reluctantly, we moved ahead.

The passageway ended at the foot of a narrow staircase.

I flicked the passageway lights off behind us. It was important to erase as much of our progress as possible.

I moved up the stairs, pressing hard against the right-hand wall. There was no door at the top. The staircase opened directly into a kitchen.

At the top of the stairs, I took a fast look, withdrew and processed what my eyes had seen, then waved Stix to join me.

We stepped into the empty kitchen. It was small, the floor filthy, the cabinetry rough. An ancient, round-shouldered fridge stood against one wall; an oven that looked like it had never been cleaned stood against another, along with a kitchen table with a pair of mismatched chairs.

Gruesome as they were, we opened both the fridge and the stove.

There were no body parts in either.

But on the table stood a clue that told us Martin Dillon had been there recently.

The kettle was full of still-hot water.

"We just missed him," I said.

"Shit!"

The teapot stood beside it.

And next to the teapot, an empty box of tea.

"But not to worry," I said. "He's coming right back."

Chapter Thirty-Five

WE HAD MAYBE FIVE MINUTES.

Ten tops.

You take this floor, I signalled to Stix. *I'll take upstairs.*

He nodded.

We moved down the hall. The living room lay to the left. He moved quickly into the dimness of that room, then waved at me, urgently.

"What's that shit?" he whispered.

The walls were covered in pentangles. Dozens of them, daubed in oil paint. Every one was upside down, point towards the floor.

"They're suppose to evoke demons," I whispered back.

"They're working," he said. "We're here."

While Stix searched the main floor, I ran quietly upstairs. We couldn't be sure Martin Dillon wasn't waiting for us, wasn't hiding in a wardrobe or beneath a bed. There were three bedrooms and a bathroom on the upper floor. None of the rooms upstairs had doors.

I checked each room carefully. It wasn't hard. The first

two bedrooms were completely empty.

The next room, the bathroom, was disgusting. The bathtub was filthy, the sink choked with hair and the toilet hadn't been flushed since his last void.

I held my breath.

I was about to leave when I noticed the medicine cabinet. I flicked open the door. The cabinet was crammed full of Martin Dillon's migraine medication. I pulled out a carton of DHE. There were five ampoules in the box.

And there were five full boxes with the telltale green and red stripes.

Beneath the DHE I saw more than a dozen bottles of saline.

And a box of syringes.

Maybe two dozen of the disgusting things.

God.

I hated needles.

And finally, on the very bottom shelf, an obscene amount of little blue Viagra pills.

I shut the door, not wanting to go there.

Martin Dillon's bedroom was a disaster. To call it a pigsty insulted pigs. The walls were covered in painted pentangles, every one reversed to evoke the Devil.

The king-size master bed sat in the centre of the room. The pillows were filthy grey slabs. The blankets lay in a heap and the sheets were stained and discoloured. A set of night tables sagged beneath the weight of pornographic magazines, books and videos.

I was curious to see what books he read.

Not wanting to touch anything in that room, I used my

foot and pushed a couple free from beneath the porn. *Many Lives, Many Masters* by Brian Weiss. Another: *Reincarnation: Claiming Your Past, Creating Your Future* by Lynn Sparrow. And a video entitled *The Bloxham Tapes.*

No real surprises there.

The only other furniture was a narrow three-drawer dresser. The drawers were wide open, clothes hanging out like the drawers had thrown up.

I heard Stix moving up the stairs.

"Eddie?" he whispered.

"In here."

"Anything?"

I shook my head, but there was still one place to look. I stared at the bed. It sat too close to the floor to conceal a man the size of Martin Dillon but there was room for Angie.

Stix dropped to the floor.

He tossed the disheveled blankets aside and laid his face against the threadbare carpet.

And jumped.

"Jesus Christ, Eddie!"

He rolled onto his knees, eyes the size of organ stops.

I dropped next to him, pushed the gun ahead of me and lay my face against the carpet.

There was something under the bed.

I couldn't be sure but it looked horribly like a body.

Maybe four or five feet long.

And a foot or so across.

It was too dark to see any definition and I prayed to God it wasn't Angie.

I pushed my free hand beneath that filthy bed and came up short.

The only way to reach it was to press myself against the greasy side of the bed. I rolled closer, extended my fingers until I felt the fabric of something give under pressure. I moved my hand down until I felt something curved, like a rope. My fingers closed around it and I began to pull it out from beneath the bed.

It wasn't Angie.

We heard the metallic clank that came from inside the canvas bag but, by then, I already knew what was in it.

"I'm gonna puke." Stix looked on in horror as I emptied the bag.

It was Martin Dillon's skull-crushing machine.

It didn't take much to slot together. Two halves of the curved, head-crushing plate slid together along an open hinge. The folding ladder extensions snapped into four holders welded to the outside edges of the crush plates. It was a thirty-second job to snap the thing together.

Not that we tried.

He hadn't cleaned it off since he'd used it to crush Gina Lansdale.

At least, I hoped to God she was his last victim.

Neither of us had the stomach to put it back in the bag. We booted it back beneath the bed.

"Shit! Fuck! Shit!" He was getting close to the edge.

"Shh!"

"Don't fuckin' shush me!" he said, indignantly.

"Listen!"

And then he heard it, too.

The unmistakable thump of a powerful V-four motor pulling into the garage at the end of Martin Dillon's garden.

Chapter Thirty-Six

WE HAD TWO OPTIONS.

Stay in the house and ambush him as he came up into the kitchen.

Or get the hell back down in the cellar and jump him there.

The second option made more sense, because there would be less space for him to run.

We took the main stairs three at a time. We were part way down the back stairs into the cellar before the V-four shut down.

We had time.

There was only one place to set up an ambush.

The empty cell.

We didn't turn the lights on and groped blindly along the passageway wall in darkness. As we reached the open cell, we heard the crash of the inspection pit cover closing behind him. Weak light leaked around the edge of the filthy carpet blocking the tunnel ahead.

We ducked into the empty cell and pressed hard against

the walls on either side of the opening. We'd had no time to form a plan. My best idea was to wait until he'd passed the cell, step out behind him and maybe fire a warning shot.

In his ass.

The best laid plans of mice and men.

We heard him approaching, splashing through the sewage along the tunnel floor. He reached the opening, threw the carpeting open and turned on the overhead passageway lights.

He stamped the sewage from his motorcycle boots on the concrete floor as he approached the open cell.

Then he stopped.

In the thin light, I could see Stix keyed up, tire iron at the ready. He was breathing silently through his mouth.

But what was keeping Dillon?

A sound.

Something scraped against the concrete.

I froze, not even a blink.

Then the lights went out.

Chapter Thirty-Seven

PITCH BLACK.

The total absence of light.

There were no degrees of darkness down there. It was a total blackout.

I could not see my hand one inch in front of my face.

I strained to hear if he'd simply forgotten something and had gone back through the tunnel.

But that wasn't it.

We'd have heard him, splashing away from us.

Now, nothing.

Less than nothing.

Something had spooked the son of a bitch. Had we left the peephole open? The lights were all off. We hadn't made a sound. It didn't matter. He was alert that something was wrong.

Or perhaps he was just being cautious.

He didn't necessarily know we were waiting for him inside the empty cell.

I worried about Stix. He was wound pretty tight by now.

Would he snap, go screaming off down the black passageway, swinging the tire iron like a crazy person?

Time would tell.

We waited.

Time passes slower in total darkness. What felt like an hour was probably two minutes.

That's when I sensed movement at the opening to the cell.

Something large.

A bulk that added thickness to the darkness.

I kept my gun arm loose by my side. I couldn't risk a shot in case I hit Stix by mistake.

Then I heard it.

It was a soft sound.

A creak.

And I understood exactly what it was.

His goddamned leathers.

Dare I risk a shot?

While I debated, I heard another sound, a faster one, something slicing through the air. Then a solid thump as Stix hit him hard across the shin with the tire iron.

And then all hell broke loose.

Chapter Thirty-Eight

HE CAME IN LIKE A BULL IN HEAT, lashing out with those great fists that felt like we were being hit by chunks of tempered steel. It was an impossible situation, lashing out in solid blackness, uncertain whom you were hitting. I holstered the SIG Sauer. It was worse than useless at that point. Every time I touched leather with one hand, I drove the other fist into it with everything I had.

He grunted, spun around, lashed out with his feet, charged us, head down, indestructible beneath the damn crash helmet. As he brushed past me in the blackness, I got my fingers under the visor, latched onto it and tried to rip it off but almost lost a fingernail instead.

I heard a choking sound.

"Stix!"

More choking.

I grabbed a great expanse of leather. It might have been his back. I aimed for what I hoped was his kidneys and delivered a piledriver.

A grunt.

I pounded him, drove six or seven more sledgehammer blows into the same spot before he let go of Stix and spun towards me. His arm caught me a shocking blow across the shoulder, threw me clean across the cell. I caught my foot on one of the floor shackles and went flying. He came after me with his feet, great heavy motorcycle boots stomping the floor around me as I scrabbled hard to stay out of his way.

I heard the clang of the tire iron as it sparked off the concrete. It looked frighteningly close. Who had it? Was it Stix or had Martin Dillon taken it from him?

Another clang.

Then another.

Then a thud as it connected with flesh and bone.

Martin Dillon roared.

In pain?

Or excitement?

He was still close and I was still on the floor. I took a chance and bought my feet together, knees to the chest, then exploded up and out.

I hit somebody hard.

I hoped it wasn't Stix because I did it again.

Then rolled, got my feet under me and stood up.

And, mercy be, the lights went on.

I stood four feet from the hulking, breathless man who wanted to tear me limb from limb. I levelled the nasty end of the SIG Sauer at his crash helmet and slipped my finger around the trigger.

"On your knees, Goddamn you."

He spat at me but most of it landed inside his helmet.

"Knees!" I yelled at him.

But the truth was, he really believed all that reincarnation shit. And he was less afraid of dying than I was of killing him. He grabbed the sides of his massive helmet and pulled it cleanly off his head. He let the strap slip down his fingers and swung it like a club. The helmet scythed through the air with a sharp whistle and he stepped forward to deliver a crushing blow.

And Stix opened up the side of his head with the nasty end of the tire iron.

His whole body reacted. His arms went up and out, his legs buckled and his helmet slammed into the wall inches from my head. When he fell, it was like watching a tree fall in the forest. He hit the ground with such an impact, his whole body bounced before rocking back down, spraying blood in a crimson fountain from the gash across the side of his head.

"Is he dead?"

Stix stood stock-still, the tire iron hanging from his hand like a pendulum. I got on my knees and found a wrist but could not get a pulse.

"Crap!" I said. Then, "Wait."

I ran my finger up the side of his massive neck, digging in until I felt the pulse strong and hard beneath the thick cord of muscle. I looked up.

"He's okay."

I'm not sure if Stix was relieved or disappointed.

Martin Dillon groaned, stirred on the concrete floor. Stix lifted the tire iron like a golf club.

I waved him off.

"Give me a hand," I said.
We only just made it.

Chapter Thirty-Nine

WHEN MARTIN DILLON REGAINED consciousness, we had barely finished shackling him to the floor of his own cell.

And he did not like it one bit.

He bucked and reared against the metal cleats digging into his wrists and ankles and we moved into the passageway in case the damn shackles broke free.

Despite his almost superhuman strength, the shackles held. He never gave up trying, but when our confidence returned, we re-entered the cell and stood over him.

"It's over now, Martin," I said. "Where's Angie?

His eyes were slits. They swivelled behind puffy, swollen lids. His face was scratched up and his lips flecked with spittle.

"Last chance."

When he finally spoke, his voice, deep and ugly, seemed to resonate within the confines of the cell.

He spoke slowly.

"Fuck you. Fuck you both."

Stix kicked him and Martin brought his head up and

spat a mouthful of blood and spittle all over Stix's shirt.

I'd patted him down while we shackled him. The only keys I found were to his motorcycle.

"Where are the cell keys?"

He swivelled me a look that needed no words.

"Take this." I handed Stix the SIG Sauer. "If he breaks a limb free, shoot it off."

"Where are you going?"

"The garage."

It wasn't a trip I wanted to make. I took a deep breath and went through the tunnel. Doubled over, I moved as fast as I could. I wasn't trying to keep quiet this time. I slammed through the inspection cover and sucked in a lungful of relatively fresh air.

And then another.

The bike was sitting on the far side of the garage. It was an old 1985 Suzuki Madura. A 1200cc V-four, shaft-driven, water-cooled beast with enough torque to reverse the rotation of the earth.

But it wasn't the bike that interested me. It was the sidecar. I found four snaps on the inside and after I popped them open, the top half of the sidecar sprang free.

The hollow bottom half was empty. But it was plenty big enough to transport a body.

Dead or alive.

I was gagging by the time I got back to the cell. We had to finish this thing soon or we'd asphyxiate. Stix was looking awful. I wasn't sure I could leave him alone with Martin Dillon much longer.

But I had no choice.

"Two more minutes," I promised.

"We don't have two more fucking minutes, Eddie!"

"Trust me, Stix. He'll tell us what we need to know."

I said two minutes but I was gone three. And when I got back, I set Martin Dillon's migraine medicine out on the concrete floor. Twenty-five phials of DHE. Plus a dozen syringes. Each phial held one cc of clear liquid. I snapped the heads off all twenty-five bottles and quickly sucked up five ccs in each syringe. Five syringes, twenty-five ccs of DHE.

Dillon watched and I caught the quick, slick movement of his tongue as it slithered fast across swollen lips.

Don't like what's coming, do you, you murderous son of a bitch?

Maybe I can't kill you in cold blood but here's something even worse.

"Maximum dose is six a week. Fifteen at once should do the trick."

"You're gonna kill him?" Stix was worried.

"Not quite. DHE is a vascular constrictor. It's very specific. It only shrinks blood vessels within the brain. Fifteen doses will starve his brain of oxygen. It'll shut him down without killing him. He'll lose control over his bladder, bowels, digestion. He'll need a feeding tube. It'll turn him into a goddammed vegetable." I turned to Dillon. "Look at me." I held up the first syringe. "Where is she?"

He looked, for a very quick second, like he might tell me. Then decided to call my bluff.

"Fuck you."

"Say good night, Mr. Potato Head."

I moved around behind him. I wasn't going to jab him

in his thigh through almost a quarter inch of leather. I grabbed a handful of hair, slammed his head to one side, ignored the blood seeping out, and buried the needle into the thick cord of his neck muscle. I didn't even let the air out first.

He squealed like a stuck pig, his big body arching clear off the floor as I pressed the plunger hard. The muscle took the full brunt of five ccs all at once. I ripped the needle out, slammed his head to the opposite side and buried the second needle to the shaft in the opposing neck muscle. I forced the plunger all the way down to the stop. I tore the second needle out, locked my arm around his throat and jabbed the third needle into his neck, just an inch from the second injection site.

Before I pushed the plunger, I whispered in his ear.

"No more boners for Martin Dillon. There's not even enough Viagra in your medicine cabinet to ever get you off anymore."

Bingo.

I finally hit him where he lived.

He went absolutely ballistic.

The floor began to vibrate and I really feared for the metal shackles. He heaved and shook violently, tearing his flesh against the wrist and ankle cuffs, screaming at the top of his lungs.

"She's here! She's here! Stop! She's here!"

So I stopped.

But I left the third needle where it was just in case.

The keys, he said, were under the staircase, beneath a loose slab of concrete.

Stix was on his feet, running. He swung beneath the filthy staircase. He ran his hands back and forth over the uneven ground.

Nothing.

"The lying bastard!"

"Slow down," I said. "Try again. Go slower."

He found them on the second try. A large piece of loose concrete gave up a set of keys. He dragged them free of the hole and we hurried back to the open cell.

Stix shook the keys in Dillon's face. "Which fuckin' door?"

For a long moment, I thought he wasn't go to tell us. But the threat of living as a sexless vegetable was too much, and he gave it up, finally.

"Green," he said.

Attached to one key was a piece of green electrical tape.

We found the matching piece of green tape on the third padlock. Stix's hand was shaking as he jammed the key in the lock and twisted it sharply counter-clockwise. He threw the padlock away and between us we worked the metal door-slide out until the massive door creaked slowly open.

"Ange!"

The cry caught in his throat. It was a heartbreaking scene. The missing door lay on the cell floor. It was barely clear of the ground. He had placed four heavy paving slabs on the door, one in each corner, and I had no doubt she was dead beneath.

We moved the paving slabs first.

"Hang on, Ange!"

Dear God.

We grabbed the door.

Oh God, it was heavy. How the hell anyone could survive five minutes beneath such a crushing weight was beyond me. We lifted together and I felt it in every muscle in my body. The door moved slowly. We lifted it a foot, then two feet.

"Don't drop it," I said.

We could see Angie's body spread-eagled on the floor.

We rested the door against the end wall and dropped to Angie's side. A revolting piece of rag had been duct-taped inside her mouth. Stix peeled away the duct tape as gently as he could. It was impossible to tell if she was breathing. He peeled the tape from her lips and plucked the rag from her throat.

She took a loud, shuddering intake of breath that scared the hell out of both of us.

"Je-sus!" Stix sat cradling her head while I undid the butterfly clamps on her wrists and ankles.

We carried her between us. We got her to the foot of the stairs and Stix took her in a fireman's lift, hoisting her up over one shoulder. We rested in the upper hallway and I phoned for an ambulance.

And put in a call to Inspector Gerry Newcombe.

I took the chain off the front door and opened it to the wall to let some air through.

Angie sat quietly, still in shock, nursing her left wrist and taking small breaths that wouldn't hurt her rib cage. Stix stared down at her, his eyes rimmed with tears.

"I should go back down," he said. "Give him the rest of that shit."

"About that," I said.

He looked at me hard.

"It wasn't DHE, Stix," I said. "It was just saline. Which is harmless. I loaded five syringes with the stuff before I came back down. I couldn't risk turning him into a turnip in case he lied. Then where would we be?"

"You couldn't tell me?" He sounded bitter.

"In front of him?"

"Ah, shit."

"He doesn't know it's saline. You could still stick him with the rest."

He laughed, a dry, hollow bark, but stayed put. He put an arm around Angie's shoulders and pushed his face into her hair and began to cry.

I reached out and took his other hand in both of mine.

And that's how the ambulance men found us four minutes later.

Chapter Forty

THEY TOOK ANGIE TO THE Great Ormond Street Children's Hospital. Stix went with her in the ambulance while I waited at the crime scene for Newcombe to arrive. We were there most of the night until I grew tired of the repetition, of answering the same questions with the same answers over and over again.

"When are you letting Dr. Maurice go?" I asked.

"When I'm good and ready," he replied.

I began asking that same question every time he asked a question of me. Pretty soon, I got on his nerves.

"You're a right royal pain in the arse," he said.

"Does that mean you're letting him go?"

He took a long drag from his umpteenth cigarette of the night.

"If it gets you off my back," he said.

I drove the Jag to the hospital around six the following morning.

By then, they had manacled Martin Dillon inside a

heavy-duty straitjacket and seven burly policemen manhandled him up the stairs. I was all for cutting him into manageable pieces but they voted four to three against me.

On route to the hospital, I got rid of the SIG Sauer.

They've a better chance of finding Jimmie Hoffa.

I parked in Visitors Parking, took the Canon Sure Shot from the glovebox and found my way to Angie's room through a back entrance, since the paparazzi were clogging the main lobby.

Angie was in bed, sedated, her arms against her sides like a little wooden soldier. Stix dozed in the chair next to the bed.

I tapped his foot.

"How is she?"

He blinked, rubbed his eyes, sat up straighter.

"She's strong," he said. "Young. She'll pull through. She's got a busted wrist. And a separated shoulder. Her ribs are bruised but nothing broken. It'll take a while to know if 'er 'ead's okay. They did an MRI so they know it's not crushed. But mentally? We'll 'ave to wait and see."

I waited, but he didn't tell me what I wanted to hear.

"He was quite the nutter, was Mr. Dillon," I said.

"You can say that again."

"They found some remains. Well, more than some. They figure he'd killed at least a dozen people in those cells."

"How come his old man didn't stop him?" he asked.

"He couldn't," I said. "According to the neighbours, the old man was bedridden. Had been for years."

I stood at the end of Angie's bed, feeling bad that I hadn't stopped to pick up a card or a bunch of flowers.

"Here." I handed him the camera. "I took a couple hundred pictures at the house. Exclusives. All yours."

He thanked me, though pictures were probably the last thing on his mind.

"I'm glad she's okay, Stix. It'd break my heart if he'd damaged her any more than he did."

The unasked question hung in the quiet air between us.

Finally, he looked up.

"Yeah. She said he did try. But she fought back. Tried to scratch his eyes out. They brought in a rape kit but she told them to sod off, said he never raped her."

"His face was all scratched up."

I think he'd forgotten that.

His relief was evident.

"I think she's probably right," I said.

We looked at each other a long moment, then he stood up suddenly and we hugged each other's brains out.

He couldn't stop crying.

"Donald bloody Trump, my arse!"

Groan. It was Stix's ex-wife, Sharon, and she probably was loaded for bear.

"About that." I tried to apologize but she waved me off.

"He told me what you done," she said. "Come 'ere."

She wrapped both arms around me and kissed me hard on both cheeks.

Then burst into tears.

It was definitely time for me to go.

"Anything you want me to tell the paparazzi?" I asked Stix as I turned to go.

"Yeah," he said, "tell 'em to spell my bleedin' name right."

Chapter Forty-One

WHEN THE NEWS BROKE, Peter's book made number two on the bestseller list. He'd elected to stay in England, moving north to complete the book tour.

Peter, Sylvia and I stood together in the front hall of the rented house. We all had our bags packed. Sylvia was flying to Canada. She'd had enough.

"I don't know what to say." Peter looked at his feet.

He turned to face me.

"I'm so very grateful to you." He put his hand out, and we shook.

"Why don't I give you two a minute?" I said.

I carried our suitcases to the gate where our taxi was waiting.

"Well, look at the state of you," the cabbie said.

I looked up as Ronnie climbed from his cab. He stood in front of me, grinning.

"I've looked better," I said. "Heathrow, okay?"

"Right-oh, guv." He scooped up the suitcases. "I've been reading about your escapades," he said. "Figure I'll get to hear them first-hand now." He paused, looking concerned.

"It's okay," I assured him. "I don't have the manuscript anymore."

"Thank the Lord for that."

The sun came out, finally, and Ronnie drove Sylvia and me to the airport. Sylvia had booked us both on the same direct flight to Calgary, saying she wanted company. Said she didn't want to fly direct to Vancouver all on her own.

Who could blame her?

I left her in the first class lounge while I used the pay phone to call Eric Glossard. I'd tried him several times from Peter and Sylvia's house but there had been no answer.

"'Ello?"

"Eric?"

"Yeah," he said. "Who's this?"

"Eddie Dancer."

"Christ. I thought you was dead."

"So did I." I paused. "I just wanted to call you before I left."

"I've been reading about you in all the papers," he said. "You did tell me you was good. Didn't think you was *that* good."

"I got lucky, is all, Eric."

"But you let that bastard live," he said.

"Yeah, well. Maybe that was a mistake."

He was quiet for a moment.

"Nah. You did what you 'ad to do," he said.

And then he told me something I really wished he hadn't.

Chapter Forty-Two

SYLVIA WAS WAITING, and I ordered drinks at the bar. When I tried to pay, the barman told me it was taken care of and nodded to someone over my shoulder.

I turned.

Detective Inspector Gerry Newcombe was standing behind me. We observed a moment of silence.

"Came to see you off," he said.

"Make sure I boarded the plane?"

He shrugged

"Summat like that."

"Well, there's not much chance I'll stay," I said. "I don't like the wet stuff."

"Who does?" he said. "Speaking of which, we found Gina Lansdale's translation. Hidden in his bedroom. It's solid, so you pro'bly don't need to come back for the trial."

"Appreciate you letting me know."

"We turned the original over to Dr. Maurice. Up to him what he does with it." He looked at his feet. "Were me, I'd burn it."

A soft chime sounded over the P.A. system and they called our flight. We remained standing. Gerry Newcombe stood close, looking out of place.

"Edward?"

It was Sylvia, waiting to leave.

Ignoring the No Smoking sign, Gerry Newcombe lit up a cigarette. Before he could put the pack away, I reached over and took one. He said nothing as I tucked it behind my ear.

But I could have sworn he smiled as I turned and walked away.

Chapter Forty-Three

WHEN WE REACHED CRUISING altitude, Sylvia and I ordered another drink and toasted the fact I was still alive. Even though I looked like death warmed over.

"So." I took a sip. "What have you decided?"

"About?" But she knew what I meant.

She sat for a while, looking deep inside, but I knew she'd already made her decision.

"When he slept with that woman," she said quietly, "he said he'd made a mistake. One mistake, but a big one nonetheless."

"You think there were others?"

"It doesn't matter." She shook her head. "Even if it was one time, it wasn't a single mistake."

She took a sip of her drink.

"It wasn't?" I said.

"No."

She shook her head again, and I caught a glimpse of the nape of her neck. She had amazingly clear skin.

"He had a hundred chances to stop," she said. "He knew

there was a chance of sex when he accepted her offer of supper. At her place. He knew she lived alone. He could have said no. He didn't have to go inside. He could have walked away. He could have left after supper. He could have made an excuse. He had so many opportunities to say no, to walk away, to leave. He could have stopped before the first kiss." She turned and looked at me. "We did."

I nodded.

"True."

"One mistake I could forgive. But it wasn't just one mistake, Edward."

She raised her chin an inch.

And that was her decision.

We drank together and watched the ocean shrink and expand beneath the porthole window. After her third drink, she called for a blanket and pillow and rested the pillow against my shoulder.

"Do you mind?" she asked.

"No."

She looked at me.

"Are you going to leave that there all the way home?"

"Does it bother you?"

She reached up and took the unlit cigarette away.

"It's a filthy habit," she said and dropped the cigarette on the floor.

She was asleep within minutes.

I stayed awake for most of the trip. I wondered if I'd done the right thing sending a copy of Marie's manuscript to Ronald Varney, the Newgate Ghoul.

But a promise is a promise and what was done was done.

Chapter Forty-Four

WE SAT WITH OUR FEET UP in front of a roaring log fire back home in my little house in Marde Loop. Cindy Palmer cooked chestnuts in a blackened pan of boiling water, insisting they tasted better boiled than roasted.

The doorbell chimed and I struggled out of the warm depths of the chesterfield to answer the door.

It was a delivery from FedEx.

I signed for it and Cindy peered over the back of the chesterfield.

"Whatcha got?"

"Dunno. It's from England," I said. "Maybe it's figgy pudding?"

There was a card inside.

I opened the card first.

It wasn't a Christmas card, but a thank-you card full of hugs and kisses. She had printed a note across the bottom, embarrassingly sweet, and asked if I really meant it about allowing her coming to stay with me some time. She'd signed it Sprog, inside a hand-drawn heart.

And the parcel wasn't figgy pudding.

It was a picture.

A full-colour photograph.

Of Mick, Keith, Charlie and Ronnie.

On tricycles.

And it was signed, not to Stix this time, but to me. Signed by all four of the Rolling Stones.

I wondered how the hell Stix had pulled that one off.

Cindy held out her hand and I passed her the card first.

"Who's Sprog?" she asked.

"Stix's daughter," I said.

She counted the kisses.

"I think she has a crush on you," she said.

Then realized what she'd just said.

"Oh, God. Eddie. I'm so sorry."

"It's okay." I kissed her a dozen times. "I think she's getting over it."

Later, after we'd eaten two pounds of boiled chestnuts that were, as she'd predicted, better than the roasted variety, we fell upstairs and rolled on the big bed, kicking off our clothes and diving beneath the covers where I became reacquainted with all the softer parts of Cindy Palmer.

And much later, after she'd fallen asleep on my pillow, I lay on my back and listened as another late-night chinook blew through the city. What was left of the snow on my roof finally gave up the ghost and trickled along the eavestroughs, coursing along the downspouts and away from the house. The wooden siding creaked as the wind gusted harder and I slipped out of bed and stood by the sliding glass doors of the upper balcony.

I thought about what Eric Glossard had told me on the phone.

"I sorta lied," he said. "About making that copy. We were in the real estate agent's office, in Meersburg, the day before we left Germany. In their back room because we needed to change Evan. He'd pooped and was pretty smelly. We had the manuscript with us, hidden under Evan's car seat, before we sewed it into his mattress. Anyway, there was a photocopier in the room. We thought it might be a good idea to make a copy. We was all alone. So we did. Maria done it while I changed the baby. We never told anybody. We didn't have much money and thought they might've billed us if we'd told them."

So there it was.

After all that, Maria never made a copy at Office Copy and Supply in Crawley. She'd merely purchased a green three-ring binder there. Meaning Martin Dillon never picked up a copy of the manuscript from the store.

So how the heck had he known about the manuscript in the first place?

I knew what Danny Many-Guns would say. He'd tell me about the seventeen ways our spirit arrives and departs this earth. He'd tell me about group consciousness and collective knowledge, about rebirth and recreation and, while he explained it, I'd nod with great enthusiasm.

But afterwards, when I came to reflect on it, I'd realize I hadn't understood a word.

I heard a small sound behind me. Tiny footfalls on the carpet. Then a pair of warm, slender arms encircled my waist.

"S'up?" she asked, her voice husky from sleep.

"Just thinking," I told her.

I felt the warmth from her cheek as she rested her face against my back.

"Wha'bout?"

I turned in her arms and hugged her.

"Do you believe in reincarnation?"

She snuggled against me.

"Sure." She spoke into my chest.

"Really?"

"D'you know who I was in a previous life?"

I thought for a moment.

"I've no idea."

She looked up at me with a goofy grin.

"Shirley MacLaine," she said.

And that made us both laugh.